THE OUTFIT

First published 2022 by Rebellion
an imprint of Rebellion Publishing Ltd,
Riverside House, Osney Mead,
Oxford, OX2 0ES, UK

www.rebellionpublishing.com

ISBN: 978 1 78108 985 9

10 9 8 7 6 5 4 3 2 1

A CIP catalogue record for this book is available
from the British Library.

Designed & typeset by Rebellion Publishing

Printed in Denmark

THE OUTFIT

THE ABSOLUTELY TRUE STORY OF THE TIME JOSEPH STALIN ROBBED A BANK

DAVID TALLERMAN

REBELLION

To My Aunt Maggie,
With Fond Thanks

And To Revolutionaries
Past, Present, and Future.

"As for death... I am sure you have seen it close up sometime in your life. Death, after all, is only that and nothing more."

Alexander Bogdanov, *Red Star*

PROLOGUE

Lenin wasn't enjoying Tammerfors: not the place, and not the conference currently being held there.

As regarded the former, Finland was at once too familiar and too unlike the homeland he'd spent so many years in exile from for him to feel altogether at ease. And wasn't it humiliating that they should find themselves gathered here, the great thinkers and fighters of the revolution to be, rather than in St. Petersburg as they'd originally intended? Doubtless it was ironic that the ferment in the capital had rendered plotting revolutions there unwise, but Lenin was in no mood for ironies.

Which brought him to the principle source of his annoyance, and the Worker's Hall here in Tammerfors, and the first conference of the Russian Social Democratic Labour Party—though in practice that meant his own Bolshevik faction, because plainly there could be no traitorous Mensheviks diluting the socialist waters. Yet even then, cleansed of obvious impurities and reduced to one harmonious mind, Lenin wasn't getting his way.

Life had taught him, through much hardship, that compromise was a weakness. It had likewise shown him the true path, whittled down from many possibilities. But socialists, damn them, even right-thinking socialists, loved to argue. Or maybe it was only Russians that loved to argue. Lenin was forced to admit that plausibly the blame lay there: when there was no topic two Russians would ever fully agree on, perhaps it was optimistic to expect unanimity on how to overthrow the centuries-old tyranny of Tsarism.

The man beside him, however, was not a Russian but a Georgian, from the bottommost tip of the empire, where it almost threatened to become Asia, and he spoke the language of Russia with a heavy accent. He had also, despite the letters they'd shared and the note of adulation Lenin had read in them, insisted on emphatically voicing his own opinions, whether or not they were in keeping with Lenin's own.

At this moment, standing outside the recently built and unpleasantly modern workers' hall, dressed in nothing but trousers and a red satin shirt regardless of the extreme November chill, the man named Joseph Djugashvili—who went by the *nom de guerre* of Koba— was enthusiastically demonstrating the virtues of the Mauser pistol he clutched in his right hand.

"See how long the barrel is?" he was declaiming. "That's part of what makes it so special. Good stopping power. Which is to say, you shoot someone, and they stay shot." He chuckled. "Important in our line of work."

At a distance, Koba was ruggedly handsome, wolfish and brooding and with a louche scruffiness that might have been an affectation and might have been an inability to afford decent clothing—and was probably a combination of both. His most distinctive feature was his eyes, which were of a peculiarly golden shade and flashed at the slightest spark of anger. Close up, as Lenin was, the story was somewhat different. Koba's face was badly pockmarked, and what wasn't pockmarks was freckles. It was impossible not to note the stiffness in his left arm, more evident because he tried to hide it, or the crookedness with which he stood, likely the results of childhood infirmities of the sort poverty tended to inflict.

All of which, to Lenin, made him a perfect peasant revolutionary, that being the best kind of revolutionary, and the opposite of the over-theorising intellectuals he was too often surrounded by. As such, Lenin had already decided to forgive the young man his infidelities, accepting that they were a product of the same youthful enthusiasm that had made him conclude that waving a gun around in a foreign country among a group of known radicals was a sensible idea.

Lenin waited for a lull in the lecture—Koba had removed the magazine from the boxy pistol and was illustrating how it slid back into place—and then tapped him on the elbow. "Might I borrow you a minute, comrade? There's a little matter I'd like to discuss."

There was no mistaking how pleased Koba was by the invitation. "For the mountain eagle of the Bolsheviks? By all means." Showily, he slipped the Mauser into the waistband of his trousers and turned his back on the crowd he'd taken it on himself to educate.

Lenin led the way, until they were out of earshot but not out of sight; let the others wonder what the pair of them were debating, a dash of rivalry was no bad thing. To his distaste, Lenin noticed that Koba had plucked a cigarette from his shirt pocket and was proceeding to light it. But rather than comment, Lenin positioned himself so that the bitter wind blowing around the corner of the hall carried the foul stench of burning tobacco away from him.

They stared at the city. Koba took a fierce drag on his cigarette and watched philosophically as a thread of grey rose toward the pristine blue sky.

"I'm sorry for my hot-headedness earlier," he said, in the faintly confrontational manner of a schoolboy who'd been taken aside to be given a telling off he knew he deserved and would contest anyway. The incident he referred to had involved him storming out in a rage and firing the pistol he'd just been showing off into the air until he'd calmed down. "But when you've led men in fighting as I have, it's hard not to get your blood up sometimes."

For all that part of him wanted to laugh at the younger man's posturing, those words were music to Lenin's ears. Truly this Caucasian bandit was what he needed, the antidote to so much of what made him despair about his fellow Bolsheviks.

"Nothing to apologise for there," he said. "I'd have gladly done the same on plenty of occasions." There was no reason to mention that he'd hardly ever held a gun, let alone fired one. "Between you and me, I was quite impressed. It's only right to find all this frustrating."

Koba frowned. "That's how you see it? But aren't we on the verge of great things? Isn't Russia at the tipping point, waiting for a hefty shove? That's my feeling!"

Lenin paused while the smoke on Koba's breath dispersed, and to pick his own words with care. "Perhaps," he said. "If it weren't for those accursed Mensheviks, and all the other traitors and compromisers. Perhaps we'd have had our revolution by now, perhaps we'd have had it a dozen times over. If we could make Bolshevism the loudest voice then, yes, I've faith that we might get it done." He sighed weightily. "But to be loud costs money. Everything costs money. Ultimately, the problem is always money."

He let his own eyes settle on Koba's amber ones, lest there be any question that this was the end for which he'd commandeered him.

There was a smugly feline cast to the curl of Koba's lips. He'd taken the hint. "Ah, well... if that's the case, I may have just the thing." He shrugged lazily, as though these were the kinds of conversation he indulged in every day. "Yes, maybe so. Myself and a few like-minded friends. I'm thinking we'd call ourselves 'The Tiflis Expropriator's Club,' how does that sound?"

It sounded like precisely what Lenin had been hoping to hear. "It's got quite the ring to it. And what exactly did you propose to expropriate?"

Koba looked thoughtful. "Oh, whatever we can lay our hands on. Boats, stagecoaches, wherever there's an easy catch to be had. The trick is not to draw too much attention."

Lenin nodded slowly, and for long enough to make clear that, this time, he hadn't received entirely the answer he'd expected. "But comrade Koba, you don't strike me as a man who's afraid of a spell in jail. We've all had our Siberian holidays at the Tsar's pleasure, haven't we? And the moment for the revolution is coming soon, as you say. Hell, it's already overdue!"

Koba's golden eyes glinted. They really were extraordinarily expressive, and it wasn't anger that glimmered there now, it was excitement. "So, you're talking about something... bigger?"

Lenin smiled what he considered to be his most conspiratorial smile. "Actually, I believe the time has come for something very big indeed."

PART ONE

ONE

KOBA HAD BEEN surprised to see Ter-Petrosian at his wedding, for the reason that he'd not invited him. Even if they were old friends, there was a brand of people you wanted at such an event and a brand you didn't, and Simon Ter-Petrosian, known to all and sundry by his nickname of Kamo, was definitely in that second category. To put it simply, the man was a lunatic.

But he was Koba's lunatic. And so, once they'd left the small candlelit church and travelled across town for the wedding supper, he made a point of singling Kamo out as soon as he was able, and before anybody had taken their seats.

"I'm glad you made it!" Koba declared. "I hardly had time to invite anyone, not even those I most wanted here. Kato had her heart set on a church wedding, and we couldn't get a priest to perform the ceremony. My papers are false, and they said they couldn't marry a man with false papers, the cowards. So, when Father Tkhinvaleli agreed to do it, we jumped at the chance, no matter that it meant getting married at two o'clock in the morning." He chuckled to himself. "What a farce! But it's done with, and word got around somehow, so my friends were here to wish me well after all."

Kamo was only half listening. Instead, he was observing Kato, talking to her parents on the far side of the cramped room, with what had to be regarded as naked hunger. "She's a beauty, a real beauty. You're a lucky man, Koba." He tore his eyes away with obvious regret. "And this is the end of our professional acquaintance, eh? You'll be settling down; no more giving Pharoahs the runaround and plotting revolutions under their noses?"

Kamo was speaking loudly, and there were those in the gathering whom Koba would prefer not to learn about his history with the 'Pharoahs'—that was, the police.

Koba caught his friend by the elbow, yanked, and said, "Don't be a fool." But he said it without harshness, and as he led Kamo to the door, he leaned closer and added, "It'll take more than marriage to put Joseph Djugashvili on the straight and narrow."

Outside in the warm Tiflis night, Koba guided Kamo toward a shaded alley. Dawn couldn't be far off, but at present he was obliged to find his way by keeping a hand outstretched to brush the rough wood of the wall. Reaching a spot he was satisfied with, where the darkness was particularly deep, he drew a packet of cigarettes from his upper pocket and lit one for himself and another for Kamo, who snatched it gratefully from his fingers.

Perhaps he ought not to be talking business on the day of his wedding, but with circumstances as they were, it had been a while since he'd had an opportunity like this, to lay bare what had been eating at him ever since those vital minutes in Tammerfors when the mountain eagle of his party had taken him to one side.

"You heard about Helsinki?" he said. "The robbery the Latvians pulled off in February? They got away with a hundred and seventy thousand roubles. We can't let a damned bunch of Latvians be better socialists than we are, can we?"

"You've got something in mind," Kamo remarked, not phrasing it as a question. They had known each other for a long time.

But actually, all Koba had was an itch, which had been growing since that conversation with Lenin, when he'd made a promise he was yet to keep. "Not specifically," he admitted. "Except that, whatever we do, it has to be bigger than what they managed."

Kamo laughed delightedly. "I like the sound of that. But will Kote go for it, do you think? He's a cautious one."

Kote Tsintsadze was the current leader of the Tiflis Expropriator's Club, a name Koba was beginning to find too glib to represent the gallery of rogues he'd accumulated. And likely Kamo was correct and Kote wouldn't be on side for an operation on the scale he was conceiving. Of course, Kamo's enthusiasm wasn't for the crime itself, nor the money it would hopefully bring the Bolsheviks, but for the prospect of action—or, if Koba was being really honest, of violence.

"I'll deal with Kote if I have to," Koba said, not altogether certain what he meant by it. Kote was a good sort, and a good enough leader. Maybe it would merely be a case of making him appreciate what was at stake. "But I'm glad you're on board, Kamo. You've always been my strong right hand."

This time, Kamo's laugh was vaguely obscene. "Then I suppose I won't be needed much from here on out, that Kato of yours is better than any right hand." He dropped his cigarette at his feet and stomped at it vengefully. "Tell me when you've picked a target, you can count on me. But now there's celebrating to be done. Are you coming?"

"In a minute," Koba said. "You go on ahead."

He watched the wraithlike shape of Kamo's retreating back and took a drag from his own cigarette, which he was scarcely halfway through. The Helsinki robbery had been gnawing at him, just as his meeting with Lenin had. They'd pulled a few minor jobs in the meantime, had sent a few not-inconsiderable donations to the party, and that was all very well, but was it worthy of the man he knew himself to be, or of the trust Lenin had placed in him? Nothing he'd done would pass into Bolshevik legend as the Latvian Social Democratic Workers' robbery had.

Koba sucked at his cigarette, took it from his lips, and stared at the red jewel of its tip. He should go inside. Kato would be fretting over his absence, tonight of all nights. Notwithstanding, something held him.

This had happened so fast, since that fateful day when Kato had confessed she'd missed her period and was positive she was carrying his child. That didn't mean the same to revolutionaries as it did to normal folks, how could it? Marriage, monogamy, all that hypocrisy belonged to the old order and would be swept away in time. Yet Kato was traditional when it came to some topics—her family certainly were—and what was it to him, anyway? The advantage of disbelieving in an obsolete custom was that it didn't matter whether you complied with it or not. And if he suspected there was nothing in him that could be called love, not the way others seemed to describe it, nevertheless he liked her more than he'd ever liked anyone. Perhaps there were worse fates than raising a child with a beautiful young bride who also happened to be a fine socialist.

Koba discarded the stub of his cigarette, ground it to crumbs under his heel—and tensed. The noise that had come from behind him was indistinct and trivial, and had no right to be there: footsteps approaching stealthily along the alleyway. He dug in his jacket for his pistol, before recalling how he'd decided that attending his nuptials with a gun in his pocket might not be fitting.

The footsteps halted, far enough away to be out of his reach. A throat was cleared, thunderous amid the blackness. A voice said laconically, "Congratulations on the day of your wedding, Joseph Djugashvili."

"Yeah," came a second voice, this one strident and self-amused, "congratulations, Djugashvili."

Koba didn't turn around. He didn't need to. He'd long ago developed a sixth sense for identifying policemen. There was a characteristic stink, an odour you didn't detect through your nostrils but in the pit of your stomach. The sole question was which stripe he was facing: the Pharoahs, the regular police who'd have difficulty finding their arseholes with help and a diagram, or the Okhrana, the secret police who were secret in name only and infinitely more dangerous.

Koba had had his run-ins with both types over the years. If this was the former, the most he had to fear was a roughing-up, because they hadn't a thing on him, and he'd give as good as he got. But if it was the latter, the possibilities were potentially less pleasant.

Best, then, to be diplomatic for the moment. "Thank you," he said.

"We won't keep you," the first voice informed him. "I'm sure you're eager to get back to that blushing bride of yours."

The second voice just snickered, apparently at the word *blushing*.

"Yes," Kamo said, "I probably should. Thanks for stopping by, though. I'd ask you in for supper, but you know how it is. Not much space for unexpected guests."

"Oh, we quite understand." It seemed the first voice would be doing all the talking. "And we wouldn't want to intrude. You'd better be on your way."

Koba hated to give this pair the satisfaction, but not so vehemently as he hated letting this stunt of theirs drag on longer than was necessary. He took a step toward the end of the alley, counting the seconds until the phantom speaker summoned him back.

He barely made it to two. "However, there is one thing we need to discuss before you go."

Naturally there was. "Oh?"

Without his noticing, the owner of the voice had followed him, so that it took all Koba's willpower not to flinch when they spoke from close behind him. "You made a deal. Maybe you've forgotten? We'd ensure you stay out of prison and you'd keep your ear to the ground and report any titbits we might find interesting. There was even mention of payment if those titbits were really juicy, because we're nothing if we're not generous. Hard to imagine anybody turning their nose up at a deal like that, now, isn't it? Yet it's us that have to come searching for you, and on such a special day as this."

So. The Okhrana. He should have guessed; all the regular police would be tucked up safely in their beds at this hour. And there was no use in pointing out that he'd kept his side of the bargain about as well as they had theirs. It had been a blatantly one-sided arrangement, which he'd never had the faintest intention of observing, and indeed, he had practically forgotten the occasion, which had merged with his many other brushes with the forces of the Tsar.

"If I'd heard a rumour I thought you'd be interested in, I'd have done precisely that," Koba said. "But as you can see, I'm a new man as of today, making a fresh start. So of course I wouldn't know anything, would I?"

The speaker made a clucking noise, flicking his tongue against the roof of his mouth. "Maybe you wouldn't," he conceded, though he didn't sound convinced. "Then again, if you don't, I'll wager you associate with people who do. The thing would be to listen whenever you're around those people and pass on whatever you pick up. Because the fact is, Djugashvili, and this is an ugly admission that I wouldn't make to just anyone, we've got our quotas. Important to look like we're keeping busy, isn't it? So we can bother you, or we can bother someone else, someone you'd prefer we leave alone, and it doesn't much concern us which it is."

Koba couldn't answer immediately. He had to wait while the white-hot fury bubbling within him subsided. What justification did these Tsarists puppets, these fucking running dogs of the empire, have to talk to him in this fashion? All right, he was still every bit the revolutionary he'd been since before he'd got himself kicked out of the seminary those many years ago, but they weren't to know that. And coming here on his wedding day was a deliberate provocation. Okhrana or no, he wondered if it mightn't be worth calling for Kamo and leaving these two a few streets away with their throats cut, as a message to others of their filthy kind.

It was once those thoughts had passed through his head that Koba realised the pair were no longer behind him—and that he could hear their footsteps receding into the night. In moments, they were gone. But the problem they'd dropped in his lap had only begun. Koba had caught the eye of somebody in the Okhrana, somebody attentive enough to discover the day of his wedding and to track him down, when he, Joseph Djugashvili, was so exceedingly efficient at not being tracked. And for the sake of his freedom, for the sake of his wife and his soon-to-be-born child, for the sake of keeping the promise he'd made to Lenin in Tammerfors, he was going to have to find a way to get them off his back.

TWO

Kamo was enjoying himself.

It wasn't often the Outfit were all together like this—for that was what they were calling themselves, the brief era of the Tiflis Expropriator's Club already a fading memory. The Outfit was a more suitable fit for the pack of revolutionary outlaws that Koba had gathered around him, a term Kamo threw about with cheerful abandon to anybody who'd listen, just as now he was gleefully sharing the tale of his recent adventures.

"So we had guns and we had bullets," he continued, "but how were we to get them here, all the way from Varna? Nearly two thousand verst, as the crow flies? Obviously, the answer was by boat: sail right across the Black Sea, how difficult could that be? Except it turned out that decent boats aren't so readily come by in Varna, not for a cargo such as that. *Shit* boats, on the other hand? Those were easy to find."

Kamo took a long sip of vodka, which he let sit in his throat, relishing its warmth, then swallowed with a tip of the head.

"Her name was *Zara*, the old hag! A name I'll remember to my dying days. She'd barely float before we got her loaded, and afterwards it seemed she might sink out of sheer bloody-mindedness. And would you believe it, her captain was a sailor off the *Potemkin*? A proper hero of the revolution, stuck with that rotten wreck! Though from how he strutted about, you'd have thought she was a battleship herself.

"I wasn't taking chances. Better a watery grave than to be caught with that little load. And if she was to go down, I'd rather it be thanks to me. I had all those explosives, and time to kill, and what else was I to do but rig her up and guarantee that, if anyone got in our way, we'd take them with us to the last man?"

Kamo scanned the small room, absorbing faces. Koba was in one corner with his back to the wall, where he could see everybody without being watched in return. Kote Tsintsadze, by contrast, was toward the centre, and the rest had found places for themselves as well as they could given the limited space available. Mikha Bochoridze and his wife Maro, who were presently Kamo's landlords, were keeping together, as were the girls, Patsia, Anneta, and Alexandra, who Kamo himself had recruited to their ranks. Those three beauties seemed to be enjoying his tale the most; Patsia gave him a wink to convey as much. The remainder, he sensed, were waiting for the punchline, or for what would follow, assuming they'd already heard how bitterly this story ended.

"But truth be told," Kamo resumed, "I'd have been glad of an excuse to take that decrepit piece of junk down with me. So you might say I got lucky when we hit the storm. At any rate, it was apparent that we were headed to the bottom; hardly an hour had gone by before she'd sprung a leak and water was pouring in. What could I do? We were nowhere near land, and everything would be ruined anyway. I triggered the detonator and cursed that witch of a tub as I did it!"

He laughed at the recollection, and a few of his audience laughed too, though it occurred to him that theirs was a less relaxed laughter, as of people wondering just what they were listening to. But that was all right. Not everyone could be like Simon Ter-Petrosian, also known as Kamo, also known as the Robin Hood of the Caucasus. Not everyone could embrace death as he did.

"Only, the detonator didn't work. I pressed it and pressed it, sure that the next time would do the trick. I was sitting there, up to my waist in water, surrounded by boxes of guns and boxes of bullets, convinced that at any second I'd be blown sky high. But no such luck! And eventually I realised my choice was to sink or swim. What good is there in drowning for guns and bullets? Fortunate that a passing sailing boat happened to spy us and pick us up." He grinned. "And fortunate that my girls there, Anneta and Alexandra, managed to lay their hands on a shipment of bombs, or you'd have been truly angry with me, Koba."

Much as he'd taken pleasure in the telling, this was the

crux of Kamo's yarn, the awkward moment of confessing in front of the entire Outfit that he'd returned empty-handed. He'd done so to Koba in private, and harsh words had been spoken, but that was one thing and this was another. If Koba should let him off in front of this gathering, that would be the end of the matter. And if he didn't...

But Koba, whose lupine eyes were glittering dangerously, wasn't the one to reply: Kote Tsintsadze got there first. "Maybe it's for the best," he said darkly.

Suddenly, he was the focus of the room, Kamo and his story all but forgotten. Or rather, the focus was on both Tsintsadze and Koba, since the latter was on his feet and peering down at the man he'd appointed leader of the Outfit. "How so?" he enquired, and the danger that had been in his eyes was in his voice as well.

Tsintsadze got up also, with the lazy motions of a cat unfolding itself from a comfortable spot. "Because what were we to do with all those weapons, fight a war? We tried that and saw how it went: the Black Hundreds, massacres, blood running in the streets. The setup we've got going on now is more profitable than that, and we can keep it up as long as we like."

The events Tsintsadze was referring to—Tiflis's transient slip into civil disobedience and an uprising that had fizzled to nothing—were so recent, yet seemed the product of another age. He'd had the discretion not to acknowledge that Koba had left before their climax, but the reproach was there in his tone. *Anyhow, what of it?* Kamo thought. *No-one can be everywhere at once.* However, he had enough gumption to keep out of this, and to be grateful he was freed from being centre stage.

Koba took a step closer to Tsintsadze. "You do know why we're here, Kote?"

Tsintsadze was briefly perplexed. "Sure I do. We're making money, sending it to high command. It's useful business, and we've been doing it well."

Koba sighed deeply. "What we're doing," he said, "is the work of the revolution. No revolution ever happened without guns and bloodshed. If that's too rich for your tastes, perhaps I chose the wrong man to lead the Outfit?"

Tsintsadze blanched. "That's not it. I fought last year and I'd fight again. But we're bringing money in and nobody's getting hurt... or nobody on our side. All I'm saying is, we start drawing too much scrutiny and where does that leave us? Back in jail, and then who'll send fat piles of bills to your man Lenin? What we've been doing is paying off, and we're fine with the guns we have." He patted his belt, from which the grip of a pistol jutted.

Koba's expression was impenetrable. But it seemed he'd lost his fervour for their debate, and certainly the fire in his eyes had died. "Maybe you're right. Yes, maybe. Better out of prison than in. Better Georgia than Siberia. Better keeping our heads down. And at least we don't have any Okhrana mutts sniffing around our heels." Abruptly, he released Tsintsadze from his gaze. "So, what little jobs can we be pulling? Let's hear what you've all been up to."

As members of the gang reeled off rumours they'd encountered and schemes they were midway through concocting, Kamo kept watching Tsintsadze. It was clear he'd been snubbed in some way, but what had really been said? Knowing him as he did, he could see Tsintsadze striving to comprehend where he'd gone wrong and what it meant.

Kamo could have explained it to him. He'd talked like a coward, and there was no room for cowardice at the head of the Outfit. They were bandits warring for a revolution, not petty thieves aiming to keep their pockets lined from day to day. Kamo saw that with perfect clarity, and Tsintsadze ought to have seen it too.

His musing was sharply interrupted by Koba. One of the speakers had snared his attention, and Kamo was pleased to note that it was Anneta, Anneta with her chestnut-brown hair and her soft black eyes, which made her appear even younger than she was. How could anyone not listen when she spoke? Yet it took him a moment to catch up with the thread of her speech, and to what Koba had just asked her.

"Go back," he was saying, "that name... what was the name you mentioned?"

Anneta looked uncomfortable in the face of his intensity. "This was at the banking mail office. You told us to hang around places like that, to flirt with the men, so I was doing that. But this one, he didn't seem very interested."

"Yes, but what was his *name?*" Koba repeated, with forced patience.

"I'm not sure. He didn't like giving me it much. I got the impression he didn't like talking to girls at all." Before Koba could prompt her again, Anneta finished hurriedly, "I think he said his name was Voznesensky."

Koba rubbed thoughtfully at the stubble on his chin. "So. Voznesensky, eh?"

"You want me to have another try?" Anneta said puzzledly. "I will, but I don't imagine I'll get anywhere. Frankly, I doubt he'd have noticed me if I'd ripped off my shirt and stuffed his nose between my—"

"No. Leave that to me. And good work."

Then, as though remembering something he'd temporarily disregarded, Koba turned to Kamo.

"As for you, I'm glad you didn't blow yourself into a thousand pieces. I'd sooner have my friend than all the guns in the world. And we have bombs, that's better than nothing." His lips twisted to form the semblance of a smile. "Now all we have to do is find a use for them."

THREE

"VOZNESENSKY! FANCY RUNNING into you here."

Caught in the middle of the bustling street, Voznesensky turned around, surprise and incomprehension flitting across his pudgy features, along with a visible effort to put a name to the face that was grinning back at him. Then... "Well, if it isn't Djugashvili! Soso Djugashvili, I haven't seen you since the seminary."

Koba winced at the childhood nickname. "I'm going by Koba these days."

Voznesensky laughed. "Like the hero from that book you used to love so much? The one by Kazbegi?"

The book, *The Patricide*, was indeed where he'd taken his name from, and this conversation was already off to an irritating start. "I'd forgotten," Koba said. "That's a coincidence! But what are you doing here, Voznesensky? Didn't I spot you coming out of the banking mail office?"

Voznesensky nodded, thankfully diverted from any further stupid questions he'd been formulating. "That's where I'm working. It's a living, anyway. And how about you, what have you been up to? I heard you'd left Tiflis long ago."

"Oh," Koba said, "a little of this, a little of that. I've never seemed to find a job that suited me. But the banking mail office? That's quite a responsibility."

Voznesensky puffed out his skinny chest. "I'm just a clerk. Still, you're right, it's a big responsibility, to be so close to so much money."

Koba slapped him on the shoulder. "It's obvious we've plenty to catch up on. I expect you won't even know I got married? Why don't we go somewhere for a drink? I want to hear everything."

Voznesensky looked abashed. "I'd be happy to, only I'm on my break. And if they were to smell alcohol on my breath, that would be the end of it. I'm sorry, Soso. Another time, perhaps?"

"It's Koba these days," Koba reiterated, with a fraction more heat. "Ten minutes, they can spare you that, can't they? And not a drop of alcohol need pass your lips, there's a milk bar around the corner. Ten minutes, a glass of milk, and then you can go back to taking care of other people's money."

Voznesensky wavered, his eyes drifting from Koba toward the banking mail office. Koba, in turn, tightened his grip on the man's shoulder, until finally Voznesensky said, "What harm can ten minutes do? Gladly, Soso, let's have a glass of milk. In fact, let me treat you to one."

Koba led the way to the Adamia milk bar and found

seats while his newly reacquainted friend bought drinks as he'd promised. Voznesensky was entirely as Koba remembered him, airy and unambitious, the sort who'd never amount to anything and would die without leaving a trace on the world. A job at the banking mail office was ideal for him; spending his hours handling other people's wealth while he himself scraped by on a pittance was the perfect role for such a nonentity.

Now the question became, how to make use of such a person? Koba had few valuable memories to fall back on, since the reality was that the two of them had never been friends and that Voznesensky had lived in dread of Koba throughout their shared stretch at the seminary, with good reason. Therefore, intimidation might be the way to go, if no alternatives bore fruit. Maybe a visit to his home with Kamo, late one night, would prove persuasive. But in general, Koba preferred to be charming, if charm would get him what he wanted. So how to charm Voznesensky?

The subject of Koba's contemplation slipped into the seat opposite and placed two glasses of foaming yellow-white milk on the table between them. He reached for his, took a mouthful, and smacked his lips earnestly, apparently unaware of the second moustache lathering the upper one.

"What I recall most about you in the seminary," Voznesensky began without preamble, "was how you'd always have your nose in a book. And it didn't matter at all whether that was a book we were *supposed* to be reading. I suspect that half the time you chose them because you weren't supposed to, isn't that so? I remember how you worshiped Zola and wouldn't give him up, even though old Father Germogen locked you away for reading him." Voznesensky let out a sigh. "I envied your bravery. All I ever got to read was the books they allowed." He brightened. "But now I'm free and I can read whatever I like! Tell me, Soso, are you still a lover of poetry?"

Koba, who hadn't anticipated this garrulous rush of childhood reminiscence, was momentarily struck dumb, but he rallied quickly. "Poetry? Of course. What Georgian doesn't love poetry?" The artform was a foible he'd largely repudiated years ago, another casualty of the revolutionary lifestyle, but he wasn't so foolish as to admit that to Voznesensky, who was patently warming to his topic.

"Absolutely, it's in our blood! It's as the poet Soselo wrote in his ode to Eristavi, *Then oh Bard, a Georgian / Would listen to you as to a heavenly monument.* Poetry is the true religion of the Georgian mind, the real conscience of its people."

Koba was glad he hadn't started his milk, because it would have ended up gushing out his nostrils, such was the force of the laugh that burst from him.

Voznesensky stared at him indignantly. "I see you don't agree. Or perhaps you find my feelings exaggerated? I suppose it *is* funny, a humble clerk imagining himself a connoisseur of poetry. But Soso, I confess that to be *laughed* at—"

Koba held up a hand to signal what he couldn't say, that he'd intended no offence. With a colossal struggle, he brought his hilarity under control. "No, no," he sputtered, "it isn't that." And now he did take a sip of milk, to calm himself. "Only that I'm surprised to come across a fan of Soselo's. He isn't widely read."

It was evident that Voznesensky still didn't understand why anyone would be amused by this. "It saddens me to hear that. Soselo is one of our greatest modern poets, and it's a tragedy that he's written so scantily. I hope against hope that he'll grace us with more of his work. Why, when I first read 'To the Moon,' I'm not ashamed to confide that I wept for five whole minutes, so deeply did it touch me. *Move tirelessly / Do not hang your head...* I felt as though the words were written directly to me."

Koba regretted sampling his milk. "Ha, ha... yes, it's a nice enough line, isn't it? But I barely remember what I was thinking of when I wrote it."

Koba had never seen the likes of what happened then. Voznesensky's jaw literally dropped, as if the muscles in the lower half of his face had ceased to function. "You... you don't mean... you can't... to say..."

"If I'd known I had even a single reader out there, perchance I'd have kept at it. But life gets in the way sometimes, between a man and what his heart insists he ought to be doing." In truth, Koba had lost all interest in the writing of poetry, which had demanded too much attention for too meagre a reward. But that was yet another thing he wouldn't be revealing to Voznesensky, especially since, if he were being truly honest with himself, he was flattered by his former schoolmate's enthusiasm.

Voznesensky, at any rate, was far from recovered. "Soso," he stammered, "this is a cruel joke at my expense. You can't expect me to believe... but then, you always were talented. My god, you're serious, aren't you? To think that all this time, there I was, admiring those elegant sentiments, and the author was someone I might proudly call a friend."

Koba just managed to keep a straight face. "It's remarkable, all right. If we'd met sooner, who knows how differently things might have turned out?" He'd decided to risk his hand. What else could he do, when fate had smiled on him so absurdly? "But it wasn't to be. Circumstances drove me onto a—dare I suggest it?—a nobler course, and after that, there was no going back."

Voznesensky swigged from his milk as though it were vodka and he was desperately in need. "Nobler than poetry? What could be?"

Koba leaned in, so that only the width of the glass Voznesensky still clutched divided them. "Look here, Voznesensky, you seem a trustworthy soul. But what am I talking about? Even in the seminary you could be relied on. And we've established that you're a sound-hearted Georgian. Between the two of us, I'll bet you'd rather see our country out of the Tsar's grip, wouldn't you? That you despise watching her people suffer? No, you don't have to say anything, it's there in your eyes."

Actually, all that was in Voznesensky's eyes was fear, most likely fear that he was on the brink of being entrapped by an agent of the Okhrana. He gulped nervously and set his glass down with a thud. "It's... true that I'm no great supporter of the Tsar."

"I knew it! How could a Georgian, and a poetry-loving Georgian no less, ever be? And since you've shown your faith in me, I'll do the same in return. The reason I don't write anymore, the reason I've no usual job, is because I'm a revolutionary—a Bolshevik revolutionary. I've determined I'll give my all, to the very last drop of my blood, to put Georgia back in the hands of her workers, men of spirit and integrity like you and me."

Voznesensky's consternation seemed to have diminished a mite at this flurry of words. "Is... is that so?"

"It is." Koba nodded gravely. "And I'm sure you understand me, Voznesensky. You're not the type who'd cower at such a statement, let alone pass it on to the wrong characters."

"Goodness no!" Voznesensky had grasped his inference, along with the veiled threat that accompanied it. "While I'm not as brave as you, I confess that I'd like to regard myself as a revolutionary as well, in my own fashion. But a different kind, a kind that..."

However, he hadn't thought through exactly what kind of a revolutionary he saw himself as. Fortunately for them both, Koba was a step ahead of him. "Guns and bombs, the constant worry that at any moment the police will kick in your door—will drag you to be beaten in a dark cell somewhere—that's not for everyone, and nor should it be. The revolution requires all sorts."

They were speaking in hoarse whispers, but Koba lowered his voice further, and endeavoured to give the impression that what he was saying had just occurred to him. "Voznesensky, I don't believe it was a coincidence that you and I met the way we have. You want to do some good for the cause and don't know how. That's right, isn't it? But perhaps you're in precisely the place to aid us, more than almost anyone could."

Much of the doubt and anxiety had returned to Voznesensky's expression, yet it hadn't altogether replaced the spark of his eagerness. "If that was genuinely the case, Soso. And if there was no danger. Don't think me a coward, but there are those who depend on me."

Koba smiled. This had been a lot easier than he'd predicted. "Danger? For you? I'd never let that happen, I swear on my mother's life. No, listen to me, you'd be completely safe. And all you'd need to do is this..."

FOUR

Stopping the Kutaisi stagecoach had been the straightforward part. A bomb had seen to that, as testified by the wagon wheel that lay nearby, trailing a tail of shattered axle. After that none-too-subtle introduction, all it had taken was for the four of them to step out, guns held high, and for Kamo to explain in no uncertain terms what the situation entailed.

Getting away with the money? That was proving somewhat difficult.

Nevertheless, Kamo thought, as another bullet whipped past his head, he wouldn't have traded this for anything. What more could a man ask for than a gunfight in the company of three beautiful girls? And what bad luck for Kote Tsintsadze that the police had picked him up days before he could carry out the job he'd been planning. Kote's misfortune was Kamo's gain, and in more ways than one. Not merely was he here in this thrilling moment, risking life and limb like a true outlaw, but Koba had made him leader of the Outfit, which he ought to have been from the outset.

Yes, Kamo was in a fine mood. But they still had to get out of this in one piece.

They'd known the coach was going to be guarded, obviously. They hadn't known it would be guarded by half a dozen Cossacks, or that they'd take their responsibilities quite so seriously. And now the stagecoach itself, currently sitting in the mud at a skewed angle, was the only thing between Kamo, his three gun-slinging girls, and them.

"Why fight for what's not yours?" he bellowed at them. "Best to head home while you're still breathing!"

All that did was stir up the incoming bullets, as though he'd poked a stick into a wasp's nest. He hadn't really expected to persuade the Cossacks; no doubt a harsh punishment would await them when they returned without their precious cargo.

Well, that would teach them to be on the wrong side of history. "On the count of three," Kamo said to Alexandra, Anneta, and Patsia. "One, two, three..."

Kamo ducked around the nearest end of the overturned carriage, took a sliver of an instant to draw a bead on the Cossacks, and loosed a couple of shots. One of them was already sprawled in the road, writhing sluggishly from the pain of the wound in his thigh. The remaining five had taken up positions behind a low earthen bank on the opposite border, having hastily secured their horses to a stubby tree. The bright blue of their jackets made them clearly visible, and made them easy targets too, as did the excess of hubris that forbade them to lie in the muck as they should have. Instead, they were kneeling stiffly, rifles protruding like the noses of mosquitoes.

Regardless, Kamo wasn't at all certain his shots had accomplished anything, nor had those of the girls, who'd leant over each other to fire a volley around the far end.

The reprisal was another hail of bullets hammering into the carriage, which was in an increasingly poor state. The Cossacks, with their powerful weapons and copious ammunition, could whittle their cover to nothing given time. And reinforcements were sure to be on the way. Insomuch as Kamo had a plan, it had involved hoping the shock of their ambush would put the defenders on the back foot long enough for the four of them to make good their escape, and he almost wished he'd applied a touch more consideration, because the odds of this not concluding well were rising at an alarming rate.

"We need to get out of here," Kamo resolved.

"Without the money?" Patsia exclaimed incredulously.

"Of course not without the money! Hurry, get it packed away. And be ready to run."

Thankfully, this they *had* foreseen. The girls were capable at many things, and transporting ill-gotten gains was among them. Anneta made a start, flopping in the mud with her legs splayed and hitching up her skirts with no hint of dignity, in a manner that would have made those uptight idiot Cossacks blush like beetroots if they'd been able to see. While the other two protected her, she began to stuff wads of bills with practiced speed into the various hidden compartments she'd sewn in her undergarments.

The spectacle was hypnotic, and it took a bullet whizzing by Kamo's ear for him to recall that he had more pressing concerns. Lying flat, he rolled onto his side, enough so that he had a view beyond the carriage. The Cossacks were slow to register him, and he got one clean shot off before they spotted him, though all it did was conjure up a plume of dirt close by them. Kamo cursed filthily and rolled back to safety, as a glimpse told him that Patsia and Alexandra were taking turns to lay down covering fire for their friend.

"That's me done," Anneta announced breathlessly, unfurling her skirts over her knees, concealing who-knew-how-many hundreds or thousands of roubles, not to mention the milky skin of what Kamo judged to be a legitimately splendid pair of legs. He felt a flush of pride. How superior revolutionary women were to the priggish housewives of the bourgeoisie! And already she and Patsia had swapped places, Patsia tumbling onto her rear and cramming bundles of cash into her skirts as Anneta peeked warily around the end of the carriage.

Kamo checked his pistol and reloaded it, thinking longingly of the scores of guns that had wound up at the bottom of the Black Sea. With those, a job like this would have been a trifling matter. They'd have been an army, and they wouldn't be wasting their time with such paltry sums, they'd have gone straight to the big haul, the one Koba seemed to be perpetually dangling in front of his nose. Always it was *any day now*, always he was teasing a little more information out of his sources, always there was permission from the party higher-ups to wait for or some other excuse or delay. But maybe the real problem had been Kote Tsintsadze. A good man, on the whole, a good socialist, yet he'd never had Kamo's zeal. Maybe this had been Koba's scheme all along, and he'd only needed Kote out of the way and Kamo in his place, so as to have someone in charge with the nerve and ability for any task.

But if that were the case, how could Koba have known Tsintsadze would find himself in jail?

A quick barrage of shots zinged around the carriage, passing distressingly near to where Kamo was crouched, and the question was swept from his head. More worrying still were the raised voices that the gunfire had camouflaged, perhaps deliberately.

"They're up to something," he stage-whispered.

To his left, Patsia was on her feet and Alexandra was furiously secreting the last of the money about her person. *Is that all we got?* Kamo thought. *Two skirts full and some loose change?* But that made him want to laugh, and he had to remind himself that theirs was a serious plight, which might soon get very serious indeed.

Reaching into a pocket, he traced his fingers affectionately over what he had tucked away there. "Everybody ready?"

Patsia and Anneta chorused, "Ready," and Alexandra echoed them a second later, having finished ramming a final handful of notes into the hem of a stocking. That done, she recovered her pistol from where she'd balanced it on the carriage's fractured running gear and offered him a cockeyed grin. The sight was like liquid flame in the chambers of Kamo's heart. She was more girl than woman, yet here she stood, a brave, beautiful warrior of the revolution. Truly this was what it meant to be alive!

A determined shout came from the enemy, and further gunshots, and under both the slosh of booted feet slopping through mud. The Cossacks were making their move.

"Damn it," Kamo muttered, and fumbled in his pocket. Then, satisfied, he cried, "Give them hell!" and strode out, pistol extended in one hand and firing.

As he'd suspected, the Cossacks were advancing en masse. And for all that Kamo prided himself on being afraid of nothing and no-one, their approach, lined up in parade-ground order and calm as could be, made a part of him quail.

He ignored it. They might look impressive, but the most well-trained individual wouldn't be able to shoot with much accuracy at a walk, and their rifles were slow and cumbersome compared with the pistols he and the girls carried, particularly at close range. Moreover, he had a last trick up his sleeve.

The Cossacks were halfway across the road, which was quite near enough. Without lowering his pistol, still steadily squeezing off shots, Kamo probed his pocket with his left hand and plucked out the second of the two bombs he'd brought. Fortunately, the fuse had stayed lit. Less fortunately, it had almost burned down; he'd misjudged his timing in all the excitement.

Kamo threw it overarm, aiming for the midst of the Cossack line. The bomb exploded in mid-air, but then his goal hadn't been to kill anyone, not really. What he needed was a distraction, and the panic that gripped the five remaining Cossacks as the bomb burst deafeningly above them was ample. Patsia, Anneta, and Alexandra seized on their turmoil to empty pistols into their ranks, and their advance transformed instantly to a clumsy rout, as they scrabbled to regain the cover they'd so recently abandoned.

This was as good a chance as Kamo and his small gang would get to escape, and to reach the cart they'd stashed nearby. "Let's get going," he roared, turning tail without waiting for a response. And as he glanced over his shoulder, his thought wasn't for the disoriented Cossacks or their frantic mounts or for the ravaged stagecoach, but pleasure at seeing the three young women dashing behind him. Even with their skirts stuffed full of money, his gunslinger girls could still outrun most men.

FIVE

THIS SHOULD HAVE been a day for optimism. Koba was on his way to the fifth conference of the Russian Social Democratic Labour Party, a meeting that would bring together the luminaries of their movement: Lenin, naturally, and likely also Krasin, Bogdanov, and Litvinov, among many others. The Bolshevik high command were gathering, and he, Joseph Djugashvili, would have his place with them.

More, he'd be there with a great gift, or the promise of one. He was confident of that, having met with Voznesensky on multiple occasions in the last few weeks, and convinced him that poetry and revolution were inextricably entangled, and that no man could love the former without helping to bring about the latter. What Voznesensky had said, Koba's other contact, Grigory Kasradze, had verified. Kasradze, who was his mother's cousin and thoroughly disgruntled with the lowly life of a bank clerk, had been just as easy to convert, and between the two of them, there could be no shadow of a doubt. A huge quantity of money would be passing through the bank in the not-too-distant future.

Huge? No, that was a trivial word. Massive. Gigantic. An amount that would make anyone's head spin, and which would buy more guns and bullets and pamphlets and printing presses than Vladimir Ilyich Lenin, in his wisdom, had ever dared dream of.

That was the gift Koba would bear with him when he arrived at the fifth conference of the RSDLP: the seeds of the grandest expropriation in the history of the Bolsheviks, of Russian socialism, of revolutionary fighters around the world. A crime so glorious that it might turn the tide of their nation's destiny.

Only, they were on to him. They were following him, they'd been doing so for days, and they were doing so now. And Koba wasn't sure he could shake them.

They knew the addresses he frequented, they knew his friends, and they knew how to keep on him, when he was doing his best not to be kept on. And while once he'd have enjoyed these cat-and-mouse games through the streets of Tiflis, today he felt a tinge of an uncommon emotion. He was *frightened*. Not of being caught, because he'd been caught before, and not even of punishment, since he'd survived enough of that; anyway, if they'd intended to take him in, they would have done. No, what scared him was that his plans would be brought to ruin. What Koba desired most was to stand as an equal among the celebrated figures of the RSDLP, or as more than an equal, as the saviour who gave his mountain eagle the prize he'd asked for, and ten times over.

Koba didn't hurry his pace and didn't look behind him. He was a picture of nonchalance. But nor did he take the turnoff he should have, that would have led him toward the station. It would be far better if they didn't learn he'd left Tiflis, and certainly he didn't want them boarding the train with him, trailing him to his destination and potentially to the conference itself. That would be catastrophic, or, given that the odds were good the Okhrana already had the bulk of the pertinent details, at least embarrassing.

This slender cobbled street was a mix of shops and houses, the majority of them rather scruffy. Koba made as though he were browsing, absorbing the various weatherworn signs and letting his gaze slide across the displays in grimy windows. Once he hesitated and then kept going, but the next time he stopped altogether and rubbed pensively at his chin. This, he felt, was not the behaviour of a man who ought to be catching a train in ten minutes.

Decisively, he stepped inside. The shop was a dry goods store, fusty and dark. A counter ran along the rear wall, behind which an old man sat, apparently dozing, though so much of his face was hidden by a combination of straggling white hair and straggling white beard that it was difficult to judge.

Past the end of the counter was another low door, which was what Koba had hoped for. He stalked over, stomping to alert the shopkeeper. As the man looked up, his creased skin puckered further into a scowl ferocious enough to deter any actual customer. "What can I get you?" he asked with profound disinterest.

Koba pointed to the door. "Where does that lead?" he said, as if it were a perfectly routine enquiry.

Caught off balance, the old man replied with barely a thought, "Into my room."

"And does your room have a back door?"

The old man squinted at him bemusedly. "What do you mean, does it have a back door?"

"I mean, does it have a back door?"

"Well, yes, it has."

"And where does that lead to?"

"Why, into the alley. Are you going to buy anything or aren't you?"

"I'm afraid I'm not," Koba said. "I've hardly a rouble to my name, you see. But in a minute, two men will come in, and they're both on an excellent salary. They'll have some questions, and probably they won't mind throwing you a little money if it gets them their answers quicker. If you wanted to reveal to them what we've discussed, and if you're lucky, there's a decent profit to be made."

Casually, Koba opened his jacket, so that there could be no missing the pistol jabbed in his waistband. "However, you should know that if they find me, sooner or later I'll be back this way, and if not me, then an acquaintance of mine. Do you understand?"

The old man's face had fallen. "I understand."

"That's good. Do what you can to keep them talking. And pray our paths never cross again."

Koba went through the low door. As before, he didn't bother to look behind him to check if the pair were observing him. He was concealed by stacks of shelves and the merchandise piled in the window, and he knew from experience that his pursuers wouldn't approach too prematurely.

Beyond the door, as the old man had said, was a single room, which served as the whole of his living space. There was a stove, a cabinet, a narrow bed, and a whitewashed table covered by a grubby cloth. A hatch in the floor presumably provided access to a storeroom for the shop. In front of the stove, in a rocking chair, sat a woman so ancient that she made the shopkeeper appear positively youthful. She peered at Koba through rheumy eyes as he went past, and he touched the brim of his hat in salute. Then he went out by the second door.

There was no yard. The door gave straight onto an alley, and sure enough, crowded roads could be seen in both directions. Rather than head toward either of them, Koba tested the door on the opposite side of the alley. It was locked, so he moved on to the next, and then to a third. When that opened, he entered. The room was similar to the one he'd just left, if perhaps marginally better maintained. A woman was tending to a child that couldn't have been more than a year old, caught in the act of jouncing them on her knee. She glanced up at the sound of the door opening, and when she saw Koba, her attitude shifted rapidly from startlement to fear.

Koba gave her a small bow and carried on. Another door led into yet another single-room apartment, and this one contained an entire family. He counted ten people, ranging in age from a couple of years to a decrepitude rivalling that of the crone he'd taken to be the shopkeeper's mother; it was tough to imagine how the space could have accommodated more bodies. This lot seemed to regard it as significantly less strange that he'd let himself into their home. Only a woman of twenty or so took any real notice of him, and all she said was, "Can I help you?"

"You already have," Koba told her, wending his way amid the throng. He spied a coat and hat on a hook and considered swapping them with his own, but decided against it, partly since doing so was liable to provoke a fuss and partly because he preferred the ones he had.

As he'd expected, the next door deposited him on a street, somewhat quieter than that which he'd originally absconded from. If the pair following him had been smart, they'd not have gone into the old man's store, they'd have taken up posts at either end of the road and kept an eye out there. But though the Okhrana had an annoying habit of occasionally employing competent men, he doubted they'd be all *that* capable. So he turned left, back toward where he'd come from.

At the junction, there was no sign of them, nor of anyone else paying him the slightest attention. There weren't even any Pharoahs around. Koba was as satisfied as he could be that he'd slipped his tail, yet he wasn't about to take undue chances. Instead of resuming his former route, he went right, mentally formulating a circuitous course that would bring him to the station while staying off broad or unpopulated streets where he'd be too visible. He could do without more diversions through people's houses.

But whether or not he'd succeeded, all he'd won himself was a reprieve. Once he returned to Tiflis, the Okhrana would find him. And as long as they could find him, they were bound eventually to haul him in. When they did, assuming they weren't versed in advance, assuming Kote Tsintsadze had kept his mouth shut, they'd demand that he give them something of value. And if he failed to, the consequence would be all of his plans up in smoke.

What was the way out of the trap he was in? Was there one? Koba pushed the questions aside, while conceding that he'd have to grapple with them again, and soon. Nevertheless, the outcome would be the same if he didn't reach the conference, and so his first step had to be departing Tiflis without reacquiring his tail. If he hurried, he might still make his train.

SIX

"YOU'RE SURE THIS is safe?" Maro Bochoridze asked, for what had to be the seventh time.

"Quite safe," Kamo assured her, with the same patience he'd exercised on every previous occasion. "Like this, they're no danger to anybody. And as I've told you, I was trained by the best, by Krasin himself."

The topic of Maro's anxiety was the box of bombs resting in front of where Kamo sat cross-legged on the floor, and which he'd elected to set the fuses to. This meant that, strictly speaking, they weren't so safe as all that, but here was a task that needed doing, and he'd hoped that getting it over with would relax him. He didn't want to think about what might be happening with Koba, about how the fate of the Outfit lay with men he'd never met, how if it was decreed that these expropriations of theirs were attracting excessive attention, they might become outlaws not only from the rest of society but from their own party.

In general, Kamo wasn't inclined to waste much deliberation on politics if he could help it. He understood that there was a different breed of revolutionary out there, those like Lenin who felt they could fight better with words than with guns, and good luck to them. If he were honest, his friend Koba was turning into one of those: wasn't he off conferring with those busy talkers, while Kamo handled the dirty work? What greater illustration could there be of their respective roles than that Koba was with the Lenins and Bogdanovs and Litvinovs, debating the revolution to be, and Kamo was in this little apartment, readying bombs he'd throw with his own hands?

"What if you did it outside?" Maro proposed, teasing compulsively at a lock of her black hair.

His ruminations disturbed, Kamo nearly snapped at her and restrained himself. Maro and her husband Mikha had been kind to him, were letting him stay with them; and Maro was certainly no coward. Thankfully, Mikha chose to intervene before Kamo had to explain yet again that sitting outside with a box full of bombs, where anyone might pass by and see him, would not be sensible.

"Kamo knows what he's doing," Mikha said. "Best leave him to it, we're only distracting him."

Maro nodded and drifted to the samovar. But rather than pour herself tea, she stood there and continued to fidget. Was it Kamo's imagination, or was there more to her concern than the explosives in her home? Indeed, now that he considered, Mikha also looked troubled. Kamo wondered whether he should stop after all, at least long enough to set their minds at rest. But he was almost finished, and he still had his own nervousness to dissipate, which the quick motion of his fingers was going some way toward doing. The danger of the task had a definite appeal. To hold an object with the potential to kill all three of them, in the knowledge that the tiniest slip might accomplish exactly that...

Kamo marshalled his thoughts. There had to be something he could say that would put an end to Maro's worrying. "It's natural to be anxious, with business like this coming up," he tried. "And then to not know whether we have the go-ahead makes it worse. But that will be resolved once Koba gets back. Those bigwigs will see sense, and we'll be done with this accursed waiting."

All he was doing was striving to persuade himself, he realised, and Maro's expression said as much. Dimly irritated, he bounced the bomb he was about to prepare in his hand and took a moment's cruel pleasure from her anguished frown.

"That's what you'd like, isn't it?" he enquired innocently. "To be done with the waiting?"

With a concerted effort, he ceased toying with the bomb and applied himself to inserting the fuse. He had five more to get through, and then this bothersome episode would be concluded. He kept his eyes lowered, praying that would signal to Mikha and Maro that, while he valued their friendship and was deeply grateful that they'd seen fit to let him stay with them, the head of the Outfit had better things to do than field their objections.

No such luck. Mikha had evidently determined that, this once, loyalty to his wife superseded fealty to his leader. "Is that what you think will happen? That Koba will be allowed to go forward with what he's planning? They say the time of expropriations is over, that the party chiefs are turning against them."

Kamo refrained from querying who *they* were. Probably Mikha had been talking with those chicken-hearted Mensheviks, and it was no surprise that they'd be eschewing the riskier side of revolutionary life. "And, what, you reckon that will be enough to deter Koba? No, he'll get this done, one way or another."

He attempted again to insert the fuse he was wrangling with, which seemed to be stuck. Perhaps bouncing the bomb had dislodged something inside it. Pausing, he peeked up at Mikha. Had Kamo convinced him not to pursue this ill-judged discussion?

He hadn't. Mikha's expression was precisely as stricken, now, as his wife's. "Is that really what he wants, Kamo? And is it wise, after everything that's occurred?"

Curse it, not one but two questions he didn't have an answer to! Did Koba want to pull off the robbery he'd been planning for months? Kamo's first impulse was to insist that obviously he did. Yet here Kamo was preparing for it, and where was Koba? In another country, down on bended knee to be instructed by Russians as to whether or not the Outfit were permitted to steal from Georgian aristocrats. If he was fully committed, wouldn't he have decided they could go to hell? They'd hardly be complaining when the money was dropped in their laps.

But then there was Mikha's second question, and what

he was referring to. "Do you feel Kote Tsintsadze was doing such a marvellous job of running the Outfit?" Kamo said.

He didn't add, *A better job than I'm doing?* Still, Mikha caught his implication.

"Maro and I don't have any devotion to Kote. But there's no avoiding the fact that he's in the hands of the police, and likely that means he's in the hands of the Okhrana. Who knows if they've broken him? They've been hanging around all of us more of late. I hate to say it, but what if Kote had the right idea? So long as we stick to the smaller rackets, those we're certain we can get away with, we can keep it up forever. Something like this, though, that they can't possibly ignore, isn't that begging for—?"

"Enough!" Kamo barked. And he was deadly serious. He jabbed with the fuse he held in one hand at the bomb clutched in the other, furious that, as with every aspect of today, it refused to conform to his wishes.

"Enough," he repeated, and if his voice was calmer, his was a perilous sort of calm. From the corner of his eye, he saw he'd stunned Mikha into silence, and that was surely for the best. What did he suppose their goal was? To make an annoyance of themselves? To be an itch so minor that the Tsar's forces couldn't gather the energy to scratch it? They were revolutionaries, damn it, and revolution meant tearing the old world to the ground and blowing it into a million pieces, so that a new world could be built on its foundations.

Kamo gritted his teeth. His temper was a dark tide that rose in him, and sometimes he was helpless to resist it, and often he didn't try to. But Mikha and Maro Bochoridze weren't fit targets for his rage, so he concentrated on the stupid, stubborn bomb and the length of fuse, which seemed to be jammed altogether. He gave the defiant bomb another rattle, optimistic that might free whatever had snagged inside. If it didn't work this time, he was truly going to—

In the moment it happened, he thought the bang was a gunshot, and shied away instinctively, only to discover that what he was endeavouring to escape was immediately in front of him. Everything had turned white, the brightest shade of white he could ever have conceived of. And as that registered, he became aware of the pain, so intense that it could scarcely be described as pain at all. A distant part of him observed that, since he'd always had an unusually high tolerance, this must be extraordinarily bad for him to be irked by it, bad enough that perhaps he was dying. Its focus was his hands, a scathing heat, as though he'd plunged them into a furnace and held them there.

Nonetheless, all of that Kamo could have dealt with. He was no stranger to suffering, and even if he'd been shot, so what? The shock was already passing, and he'd have liked to laugh this off—yes, laugh, to reassure Mikha and Maro and to show them what kind of a man he was. He would have, too, except for one thing, that instead brought from his lips a strangled cry of horror no amount of courage could restrain. Because worse, far worse, than the searing pain was the realisation that he couldn't see.

SEVEN

THAT KOBA HADN'T noticed anyone wasn't to say they weren't there to be noticed.

His sixth sense was being dull today. Had his time abroad blunted its edge? His urge was to hurry onward and hope it hadn't failed him, but he forced himself to slow, to ease away from the mass of traffic. Stopping before a chipped window pane, he fussed in a pocket as though rummaging for some possession, while studying the skewed reflection in the glass. His view was limited to the scene directly behind him, and included a great many people, along with a couple of laden donkey carts, all of them in eager motion. Nobody was obviously heedful of him. It was as if he'd returned to the city a stranger, forgotten even by its agents of law and order.

It had only been two months since Koba had left Tiflis, yet the place felt different: smaller, somehow, and more provincial. But, as he'd wandered from the train station, dodging and shoving through the crowds, he'd recognised that it was he who had changed. These two months had broadened his outlook, had affected his priorities. His trip to England, and ultimately to a church in a region called Hackney in the city of London, had opened his eyes. The fifth congress of the Russian Social Democratic Labour Party had been a splendid occasion, with both Bolsheviks and Mensheviks together, and representatives from the Polish and Latvian socialists: three hundred and thirty-some delegates in all, at an event which had galvanised that nation's media, not to mention its police force and the local branch of the Okhrana.

Koba had viewed himself as a socialist and revolutionary for such a very long time, since he'd pored over dog-eared copies of Chernyshevsky and Marx in the seminary. But those words had been endowed with specific meanings, and those meanings seemed petty and quaint compared with the conceptions he presently held. More than ever, he could appreciate that Georgia was one battleground in a vaster struggle. And where once he'd been glad to be regarded as a country bandit, or perhaps as a proletarian thug better at muggings and extortion than at writing speeches and giving orders, now that perception nettled him. He understood clearly that he was capable of greater things, and there had been moments in London when he'd been positive others had seen the same—that Lenin had.

However, their spell in England had ended with conspiratorial gatherings, darkened by a cloud of awkwardness and suspicion. In public, the Bolsheviks had agreed that expropriations were an embarrassment to the cause, that they did more harm than good. Privately, they'd acknowledged what Lenin had conceded freely in Tammerfors: that the party was desperately in need of money. No-one was proud to admit it, and no-one was proud that admitting it required making use of the bandit leader from the Caucasus and his gang of thieves and killers. Yet when it came down to it, a lack of pride had not been enough to keep them from granting him the permission he'd sought, their consent for the crime that would immortalise his name and save the Bolsheviks from ruin.

Koba had got what he'd wanted, what he'd left Tiflis in aid of. And now he was back and he barely wanted it anymore.

But did that matter? If their grand job wasn't the be-all and end-all of his existence, let it be a stepping stone instead. That gave him more reason to ensure its success, not less. Maybe their haul wouldn't be the gift to an adored hero he'd originally intended, but the payment that bought his entry into the inner circle where he belonged. This way, he'd help the party twice over, for wasn't he wasted at the bottom of the empire, fighting trivial battles when the war might be won elsewhere? London had shown him a lot, and one truth he'd learned beyond dispute was that the qualities he brought were rare: not just a strategist's intellect, but the tenacity and bloody-handed experience to carry any strategy through. And they were rarest in men who were more inclined to write essays and withering retorts than get among the workers they claimed to champion.

So yes, there was ample reason to continue. And there was ample reason for caution, too; Koba knew they'd been watching him in London, or anyway that they'd been watching everyone and couldn't have missed his presence. He had obfuscated his journey here, although it wouldn't take much imagination to suppose that Tiflis was his eventual destination. If he were the Okhrana, and if he were determined to keep track of one Joseph Djugashvili—also known to go by Koba, Soso, and a dozen other aliases—he would have had a man looking out at the station.

Frustrated, Koba tried again to tap those mental powers he'd half convinced himself he possessed, and which might as easily be called paranoia. Well, he'd rather be paranoid and out of prison than the alternative. If Kote Tsintsadze had been a dash more paranoid, probably he'd be faring a good deal better than he was. But Kote was a subject that Koba preferred not to give too much thought to, and the prickling in the back of his mind which advised him that he was being observed or followed or that someone was other than they appeared to be was nowhere to be found.

Turning, Koba made a show of smoothing the flap of his jacket and fiddling with the band of his hat, as though hunting for a perfect angle that eluded him. In the meantime, his eyes darted to left and right. Still nothing. He felt almost resentful. Could it really be that they'd forgotten him in his brief absence? Was he no longer a priority? If so, there was one more motive to bring his plans to fruition. This might be the last job he pulled in Georgia, and it would certainly be the biggest. Let them curse themselves for ever imagining Koba Djugashvili was a man to be neglected.

He abandoned messing with his hat. Either they genuinely had lost interest in him or they'd got subtler while he was away. Most likely, they knew enough about him to predict his movements and believed they could pick him up at their leisure. Which, as he set off into the tumult of the street, raised a confounding quandary. Where was he to go? Did he dare head home to Kato? Or ought he to delay until he had a better picture of how the land lay?

By the next corner, he'd made his choice. He needed information: needed to establish what had changed, who'd been arrested or released, how enthusiastically the Pharoahs and Okhrana had been making life difficult for the bold revolutionaries of Tiflis. But more than anything, he needed to unburden himself of the news that was burning in him; to find Kamo and tell his friend that, after all these months of preparation, the time had come to make their move.

EIGHT

KAMO DIDN'T OPEN his eyes at the clump of feet on the stairs, nor at the knock on the door. People were always coming and going to the Bochoridzes' apartment, and sometimes those comings and goings involved Outfit business and often they didn't, but there was little he personally had to deal with. Maro had become inordinately skilled at diverting all except the most insistent callers and all except the most vital news. In many ways, she'd become the Outfit's substitute chieftain, a role Kamo was happy to cede to her, because she, out of everyone, seemed to covet it least.

So he lay back on his bed and kept his eyes shut and stared at the familiar darkness, as the knocking continued and was echoed by the tap of footsteps, which he recognised as Maro's since her tread was lighter than her husband's. He'd had time to learn such differences, which once would have passed him by. He heard her muffled query, but not the door opening; she wasn't so incautious as to let anyone inside without knowing who they were. However, when an answer came—that Kamo didn't catch—it was instantly supplanted by the sound of her scrabbling at the lock.

Then Kamo heard Koba's voice.

Maro replied. He thought she murmured, "He's not well enough," but couldn't be confident because his heart was pounding so fiercely. He'd anticipated this reunion, had practically craved it, and now that it had come, he felt sick with dread. Was he afraid Kamo had been ordered to call off their plans, or that he'd been given the go-ahead? He couldn't even begin to say.

Kamo resolved to focus on a task he could do, and so he made himself sit up, though sitting was onerous. He heard heavy footsteps approaching, the inner door opening, and the footsteps again, much louder. There were two sets: Maro had followed Koba into the modest second room in which Kamo had been sleeping. But a snapped word from Koba deterred her, and the inner door closed, leaving Kamo alone with his leader.

Now he did open his eyes, or rather his eye, the one not buried beneath a mound of gauze. Koba looked haggard, and thinner than when he'd left. And he also looked angry. "Who did this to you?" His tone said that, whoever they were, they wouldn't see the end of this day, which would have been reassuring under other circumstances.

Kamo made another attempt to shrug himself up against the wall. "The thing is, Koba," he confessed shamefacedly, "I did this to myself. The bombs... I was setting the fuses, and I don't know what happened, one detonated in my hand, it must have been faulty or else it would have taken my head clean off. Nevertheless... well, a faulty bomb's still a bomb." He brightened. "But here's a miracle for you! The rest are fine."

This had been a considerable source of comfort to him in the aftermath of the incident, as he'd wrestled with the possibility that he might be crippled, that he might lose the sight in one eye. Yet Koba's expression attested that he wasn't half as pleased.

"Oh, the rest are fine, are they?" he snarled. "I come back to find the man I appointed leader of the Outfit swaddled in bed, a feeble invalid, weeks before the biggest job we've tackled, but at least we have bombs we can't use." His fingers were twitching with a steady rhythm, as though he were eager for something to throw—or as if, at any moment, he'd pull his pistol from his belt and finish what Kamo had inadvertently started.

"That's not true," Kamo said, more sheepishly than he'd intended. He cleared his throat. "According to the doctor, I'll soon be up and about. Mostly it's just bruising, and he thinks I won't lose the eye. There's really nothing to be concerned over."

Koba looked for somewhere to sit, and since there was no chair, slumped onto the end of the bed, compelling Kamo to hoist his legs up. Koba took off his battered hat and played with it violently, removing dints with several sharp slaps. When he spoke, it was in a dull monotone.

"That's it, then. Two-bit crooks is all we are and all we'll ever be. That's the truth of it, and you saved us from discovering that truth a harder way, so I suppose

I ought to be thankful. Better to fail before we could show ourselves up, eh? Now you should rest, Kamo. Rest for a week, a month, a whole year if you need to. Don't worry, you'll be taken care of. The Outfit takes care of its own."

Kamo had begun to suspect that this dry monologue would go on forever, but there Koba stopped and lapsed into a profound silence and a supreme stillness, like some mechanism in him had wound down. His face was in deep shadow, and it seemed to Kamo that Koba himself was the origin of those shadows, and that if and when he moved, they'd spill around the room as water would from an upturned pail.

Kamo knew with a peculiar certainty that everything was on the line. Koba hadn't merely been venting, he was ready to scrap the job, or at best he would pick somebody else to take Kamo's place. And if that were to happen, what would come next? Would he be demoted? Or would he go the way of Kote Tsintsadze, into the cells of their enemies and the interrogation chambers of the Okhrana?

A treacherous thought, in both senses. It had come to Kamo out of nowhere and it voiced a treason against his friend and master that he'd never have chosen to admit. He'd have denied it if he could, would have rejected any possible chain of connection between Koba's anger at Tsintsadze and Tsintsadze's subsequent arrest. But for all his striving, he couldn't put this venom-whispering snake back into its box. Tsintsadze had failed and had suffered accordingly. He too was failing, and who could say what would befall him?

That made Kamo's decision, though *decision* was a grandiose word for the flood of impulses that overtook him then. He went to tear at his bandages, the gesture proving less dramatic than he'd have liked, as he was forced to begin with the sling impeding his left arm. But he succeeded, and used both hands together to start on the cocoon that was his head. Every clenching of his fingers made the left hand throb, as every pressure on his brow or cheek sent miniature lightning bolts plunging into his brain, but he toiled frenziedly, oblivious to Koba, to anything that wasn't ripping free swirling strips of white cloth. He yanked until it all came away, and then, not hesitating to consider what he'd done, he pulled off the blankets and swung his legs out. Committing every iota of his being to this one deed, Kamo got to his feet.

He could no longer ignore the various messages of complaint his body was providing. As ever, the pain was easy to disregard, and he'd never been more grateful for that strange tolerance of his; what he couldn't put aside was the actual damage, and he'd sustained plenty of that. No matter how vigorously he insisted, his body wouldn't work properly just because he demanded it should.

The vision from his maimed eye was distinctly blurry, enough so that it interfered with his unmarred eye, and the combined effect was like squinting through a window smeared haphazardly with grease. It was disorienting, and Kamo's instinct was to clutch for support. He resisted, correcting his imbalance with another mammoth effort. He planted his feet squarely and stood to his full height, contorting the bruised muscles of his face into what he imagined to be his usual devil-may-care grin.

"Koba, old friend," he said, "you're worrying over nothing. I can't blame you, it must have been quite the surprise to find me this way. I'm sorry. I'm an idiot. But look, I'm virtually mended, and when the time comes, I'll be as good as new... better than new! I'm the man for this, you'll see. We'll empty their coffers down to the last rouble, and a hundred years from now they'll still be telling tales of our exploits. Just give me a chance, won't you?"

Kamo had been so sure that his sensational display would dispel that frozen instant of crisis he'd felt himself caught in. But no, the shadows clung obstinately around Koba. Then he glanced up, and the light from the lamp beside the bed fell on his features, and instead of a single block of gloom there were only specks scattered in black constellations across his pockmarked skin.

"Fine," Koba said, not sounding impressed, as Kamo might have expected, but weary, like a parent enduring a boisterous child. "We'll keep to the plan. I'll speak to my contacts, find out the date. And you can lead the Outfit, Kamo. But I hope you know what that means. Whatever comes of this, it's on your head."

NINE

Kato was talking, but Koba wasn't listening. Probably she was talking about the baby, who was crying. Little Iakob had been in the world for three months, and much like his father, he was quiet more than he wasn't, but when he chose to make his presence felt, he ensured that no-one could deny him. Currently he was screaming fit to shake the rafters, and Kato was talking, in a somewhat desperate, fluttering manner, and Koba was doing his best to ignore both of them at once.

The robbery was days away. The pieces were in place, and all that remained was for the date—and their money—to arrive. Rather than be excited, Koba grew ever more indifferent. It was as though he was trying to devote his attention to an event in the distant past, and any questions of its success or failure were irrelevant.

The outcome was predetermined, and he had forgotten it, since it had ceased to matter.

Odd to think that a goal he'd been pinning his hopes on for so long could become so trivial. But hadn't that happened often enough before? He'd turned his back on his education at the seminary, which had meant everything to his mother and therefore to him, and then on poetry, for which he'd held such an outrageous passion. Would there be a time when socialism failed to inflame him? Would these feelings he had for Kato dwindle and dim? Would his boy lose the niche he'd carved in Koba's heart the day he'd first seen his round, red-cheeked face? Would this life of his come to have no meaning, and was it happening already? Was that why he found it impossible to focus on his wife's bids at conversation?

No. Not that. Not yet. He'd simply let himself sink into a funk, and that was something else that had happened often before. Conceivably he was anxious about the robbery, and this detachment was the way he'd come up with to process that. He'd go for a walk, he decided, and clear his head, as increasingly he did most nights. Koba got up from his chair, ambled to Kato, clasped her pale chin between his palms and kissed her soundly on the lips. "Don't fret," he said.

He continued to the crib in the corner, picked up Iakob, and awarded him also a smacking kiss upon the forehead. "And you, shush. Can't you see how you're bothering your mother?" He put the baby back and tucked the scrap of blanket around his pudgy body.

Miraculously, this did the trick. Iakob peered up at him

in stunned surprise, gurgled, and then closed his eyes and rolled over with a last weak kick.

"I'm going out," Koba declared, feeling he'd earned the right as both a loving husband and able father. And not waiting lest Kato should argue, he hurried through the door and clattered down the stairs in the hallway three at a time, until he was into the night-shrouded street.

He walked briskly, as was his custom. He liked Tiflis better after dark, when the air still clung to its warmth but wasn't so humid as in the day, and when the worst of the city's bustle had surrendered to the more relaxed mode of carousing and singing and bickering that constituted Georgian nightlife. He could have been tempted to go drinking, or to seek out Kamo or another member of the Outfit. But Kamo would persist in asking questions he was unwilling to answer, and even if Koba found someone else to drink with, they were bound to be a socialist, because all his friends were socialists, and everyone had wind of what they were up to. In a place such as Tiflis, secrets had a tendency of changing into rumours that spread like wildfire.

And, Koba thought, too late for the acknowledgement to do him any good, those rumours frequently reached the wrong people. Like the two figures in long overcoats and black felt hats who'd stepped out in front of him and now barred his path. He could have shoved past. Instead, he turned casually and prepared to head back the way he'd come. As he'd predicted, two more men, dressed in similar fashion, blocked his course in that direction, and were approaching at a rate that squared the difference between *leisurely* and *intimidating*.

They were here for him, and they weren't here solely to threaten. This was something more tangible. Maybe he ought to have been frightened, but fear wasn't in his nature, not since the first time he'd stood up to his brute of a father and discovered he could do so without the slightest trembling. Thus, he held the gaze of the men who approached, letting his mouth slip into the hint of a sneer to make clear his contempt.

The approaching pair had almost caught up. Koba didn't recognise either of them, but that didn't signify much. He wanted to curse them to their faces for coming for him like this, in public, where anyone might see. Did they propose to get him killed? Perhaps they were serious enough, and the fate in store for him was severe enough, that they were unconcerned with such niceties.

"Come on," the one on the right said peremptorily.

Then they were sweeping him along, Koba boxed in amid the four of them. They passed down three streets, and toward the end of the third came to a halt at an open-topped carriage, where a fifth man was hunched in the driver's seat. One of the four conveyed to Koba with a tilt of the head that he should get inside, which he did. The two who'd approached from behind him took the opposite seat and the other two were left on the curb as the carriage jolted off.

They maintained a hectic pace. Having travelled for five minutes, the driver pulled up, and the pair who'd silently accompanied Koba got out and waited as he did likewise. Inspecting the building they'd stopped at, he mentally labelled it as *nondescript*. This was a region of apartments, neither especially poor nor particularly luxurious, and nothing about them suggested they were a resource of the dreaded Okhrana. He could have memorised the address, had he wished to, they'd made no effort to hide it; but then, they didn't care. In their minds, he was no threat to them, and they were probably correct.

One of the two that were escorting him opened a door—it was unlocked—and trudged up a flight of stairs and another, to a landing at the summit of the building. A further four doors led off, and the man selected the nearest and knocked, hesitated for a count of seven seconds, and let himself in. Koba followed promptly, hands stuffed into pockets. He had the sense that the man's partner, who was close behind them, would have been glad to provide some physical encouragement, and Koba refused to give him the satisfaction.

The room beyond was sparsely furnished, containing a circular table, three chairs, and a new-looking samovar on a stand in the corner. An urge made Koba scan the bare floorboards for stains that might indicate where blood had been spilled and cleaned up, but they were so generally grubby that it was hard to make out anything conclusive. A man older than the rest of them occupied one of the chairs at the table. He was in late middle age and his sable hair had greyed at the wings. His face was aquiline and his eyes, in the lamplight, were positively ebon. Koba didn't know him, yet certain facts were plain: his neatness of dress and demeanour marked him as significantly higher in the Okhrana's ranks than his colleagues. What this meant for Koba was more ambiguous. The man was definitely trouble, but there was no way to establish how much or of what sort.

The officer motioned to a free chair, and Koba reckoned it would be healthier to sit without the assistance of the pair still hovering nearby. He made a point of drawing the chair out so that he could stretch his legs, and lounged with the truculent air of someone baffled as to why his liberty was being interfered with so maliciously.

"My name is Mukhtarov," the Okhrana officer said. "And you are Joseph Djugashvili, who uses the *nom de guerre* of Koba."

He didn't say this enquiringly, but it wasn't altogether a statement either. It wasn't as though the Okhrana weren't known for making preposterous mistakes, for dragging in the wrong person or accidentally combining two records. Koba, who'd made a habit of studying them as they studied him, had come to the conclusion that they were somehow both highly efficient and thoroughly incompetent, and could veer from one extreme to the other in a heartbeat. If they would only be consistent, they'd be substantially easier to manage.

He might as well keep cooperating until they gave him a reason not to. "Yes, I'm Joseph Djugashvili. As for Koba, I don't go by that these days. Some of my old friends call me Soso, and for a while I wrote poetry as Soselo. Perhaps you've heard of my work?"

Mukhtarov had a sheaf of papers open before him in a cardboard binder. The handwriting was tiny and crabbed and Koba couldn't read it upside down, but he assumed it referred to him, or at least that he was supposed to believe so. Mukhtarov consulted these papers, scrunched his brow as if he were confirming a crucial detail beyond any doubt, and said, "Our files show that you still make use of the name Koba. This will go better if you're honest."

Koba shrugged. "I'm always honest. But who can control what others call them? Names stick, even once they've been outgrown."

Mukhtarov evidently didn't feel this assertion was worth debating. "You're here because you're going to help us," he said. "You've been useful before, and now you're going to be yet more useful."

"I don't see how," Koba replied. "That life is behind me. I've a wife. I've a son. Do you think I'd risk bringing strife down on them? Well, maybe you do, but I've told you I wouldn't, and I'll tell you a hundred times if need be. Why waste your evening with me? There are real hoodlums out there, types who'd like the Tsar and everyone who takes his side up against a wall. Whereas I just hang around with some people, and barely that anymore."

He might have kept on in that vein. Mukhtarov didn't seem inclined to stop him from rambling. But Koba couldn't quite persuade himself that his lie was being accepted. If it had got back to them that he'd attended the conference in England, the fabrication was futile. Then again, there was a reasonable chance it hadn't. He'd been one straw in a large haystack, and even if that weren't the case, the various branches of the Okhrana were notoriously abysmal at communicating. If a report had been filed, that wasn't to say it would have made its way to the local office or had actually been read.

Mukhtarov had been watching him all the while, with a steadiness that might as easily have represented patience or disinterest. He had a lassitude about him that implied this was a job he'd be continuing throughout the night, with an interminable stream of visitors like Koba, and he was measuring out his energies carefully.

Now, however, that vanished in an instant, so that suddenly he was sitting straight and his scrutiny was intense. "We know a major robbery's coming up," Mukhtarov affirmed. "We know it will involve the Tiflis bank. We know the date and the location. What we need from you is the name of the ringleader."

All of this he said with perfect aplomb. Indeed, he'd spoken as one picking highlights from a vast pool of revolutionary activities that he could dip into as he saw fit. It made no difference. The man was lying. A small reveal was that he'd said, *It will involve the Tiflis bank.* If he knew the specifics, and believed Koba did also, what gain was there in being vague? No, the most they had was whispers and theories, a cobbled-together picture riddled with blanks they hoped he'd fill.

The question was, how much of what Mukhtarov had claimed was true? But on that question, everything was riding. Give away too little and they might keep him all night, all week, all month. Give them too much and not only would Koba sink the plan, he'd expose himself as its architect. But he surely had to give them something. They'd shown their hand, and they'd require him to do the same, otherwise their biggest accomplishment would have been tipping him off as to precisely what they had, or hadn't, uncovered regarding an upcoming crime.

Koba nudged himself nearer to the table, where he placed both palms flat on its surface. He leaned forward conspiratorially, bridging the gap between him and Mukhtarov, and lowered his voice, as if afraid the pair behind them would eavesdrop.

"So you know all that, eh? Then perhaps there's no point in my staying quiet. It's tough to avoid hearing things, even when you'd rather not. These socialists, none of them can keep their mouths shut; I've caught bits and pieces simply by having my ears open." Koba reclined a fraction. "Obviously I'd want to ensure my family and I will be safe. Nobody likes being picked up this way in the middle of the night."

Mukhtarov nodded lethargically. "Give us what we need and I guarantee you this won't happen again." He selected a spot on the page in front of him and rubbed at it with a finger, as though he might thereby erase some unfortunate particular. "Maybe we could do better than that. The more useful you are to us, Djugashvili, the more we can be useful to you."

Koba nodded too, and with surety, to impart that this was the assurance he'd been waiting for. "You're already aware," he said, "that it's set for the morning of the twenty-sixth, that's not news."

While he hid his reaction well, Mukhtarov's countenance betrayed to Koba that he hadn't known even that much. But that was fine. They'd still need substantiation, and they'd have an impossible time getting it, because Koba had been using his web of contacts to put out false intelligence for weeks. This, he'd long since learned, was his greatest weapon against the Okhrana. The trick was not to strangle them with too little information, but to drown them with an overabundance.

The next part was the real gamble. To protect himself—and so the robbery, the Bolsheviks, his entire future—necessitated offering up some vital snippet they couldn't acquire elsewhere. And it had to be of genuine worth, sufficient to make him valuable enough to tread lightly around.

Still, it was with a heavy heart that Koba said, "But as to the matter of who's leading it? That I may be able to help you with."

PART TWO

TEN

THERE WAS SOMETHING in the air.

David Sagirashvili knew Tiflis well enough to be certain of that much. But perhaps if he'd been merely a normal citizen, one of those going about their business around him, he'd have mistaken this for a day like any other. Were he not part of the city's revolutionary underground, a socialist and a freedom fighter, he'd have lacked this sense that alerted him, as though he were a dog responding to a frequency too high for its master's ears.

There were a great deal more Pharaohs in evidence, and armed Cossacks also. Hardly a street corner was devoid of them. But that wasn't so extraordinary, given the rumours over the last weeks, which had recently heightened to fever pitch: the claims that the Bolsheviks were going to pull something big, a proper 'spectacular.'

He'd half expected to be approached himself, as many in his acquaintance had been. Whatever that *something* might be, it was so large that one group alone couldn't hope to manage it.

Or that was how the rumours went. Yet on the face of it, the region surrounding Yerevan Square was as it always was, which was to say, busy and loud and alive with the peculiar energy that characterised Tiflis. The day was glorious, the sky a dreamy porcelain-blue canvas upon which the sun was pinned like a silver medal. On one side of the square, a clutch of stalls had been set up and were selling iced cups of fruit juice or plates of highly seasoned bean stew, and through its middle a caravan of donkeys and camels were wending unhurriedly, the drivers scowling and cussing at any traffic that declined to clear a path.

Yerevan Square, and Tiflis in general, was especially lazy on a day such as this, a day that seemed to call specifically for laziness. Watching those who strolled and loafed and chattered around him—who weren't just locals but Persians, Chechens, Armenians, and others, almost all flamboyantly dressed—Sagirashvili had difficulty in crediting what his gut insisted on and what no end of backroom talk had corroborated.

However, even if one could ignore those extra police, there was the atmosphere, which was subtly off in a dozen different ways. There were the details that were amiss, and there were those, he noticed, who loitered but weren't engaged in conversation or visibly very relaxed, some of whom he recognised. He might have paid them more attention, might have thought to look for telltale bulges in the pockets of their coats, but he had places to be, and anyway, it was best not to wonder too much. Men carried guns in Tiflis all the time, often openly, despite the violence and brutal reprisals of the year before last.

He might also have paid more attention had he not been distracted by a beguiling spectacle: the two girls who at that moment were alternately cheering on and inciting the exploits of a cavalry captain on horseback. Both of the girls were exceedingly pretty, dark haired with eyes of black, and each bore a parasol folded beneath her arm. As for the captain, he made a striking figure; his moustachioed face was undeniably handsome, if rather roguish for a military man, and the eyepatch he wore at a rakish angle gave him an air of mystery that had evidently captivated his audience. To keep their interest, he'd taken to performing tricks on his mount, and to waving a Circassian sabre that could have caused them a nasty injury had he made the slightest blunder.

As Sagirashvili drew nearer, the assembly broke up, with a patter of flirtatious laughter on both sides. Saying their goodbyes with blown kisses, the girls strutted off across the square, twirling their parasols in half-hearted synchronicity. Their objective was in the direction of the military headquarters, where no doubt they intended to find more handsome officers to tease.

Sagirashvili chuckled softly. On such a day, it was hard not to love Tiflis, and no atmosphere, no police or rough-mannered Cossacks, could diminish that. But he wasn't here to amuse himself. Quickening his pace, he continued toward the Tilipuchuri tavern, that most notorious of institutions, where princes and pimps mingled and where only a fool would conspicuously flash their money around.

As he came close and the crowds parted, Sagirashvili noted a man by the door, standing as if on guard. Sagirashvili identified him as Bachua Kupriashvili, and greeted him warmly, one brother revolutionary to another. "May I come in?" he asked, though to his knowledge, Kupriashvili had no affiliation with the Tilipuchuri and no right or reason to bar his way.

But Kupriashvili didn't attempt to do so. Instead, he grinned and gave a sweeping bow. "Of course, of course." Stepping in ahead, he grabbed an adjacent chair and drew it out, as a waiter might. "Come, sit down. Won't you have a glass of wine?"

Sagirashvili nearly pointed out that he hadn't come to drink, that he had an appointment with a friend who owned the shop above the tavern. Yet it would have been bad manners to refuse, and in any case, he suspected there was more to the invitation than simple Georgian courtesy.

He took the seat he'd been offered, took up the glass that waited ready too, and sipped gratefully. It was good to have free wine to drink on a hot day. He drained the rest in a single draught, made to get up—and saw the look Kupriashvili was giving him, the one that informed him it would be better for both of them if he stayed where he was.

Sagirashvili realised then what ought to have been obvious from the second he'd entered: Kupriashvili was not alone. The Tilipuchuri always had more than its share of revolutionaries, it was that kind of an establishment, but now there was virtually no-one else. And the few regular customers Sagirashvili made out appeared distinctly uncomfortable, with the same sort of discomfort that was creeping upon Sagirashvili himself.

Kupriashvili wasn't alone, and he also wasn't the only one standing guard. There were more of them scattered near the entrance. As Sagirashvili had just discovered to his cost, those guards weren't there to keep anyone out. They were letting people into the tavern, but they weren't allowing them to leave. His intuition had been right, but his timing had been all wrong, because whatever the Bolsheviks were up to, it was happening now.

ELEVEN

THE TIME WAS almost on them. Kamo had already dismounted, and for the last minute had been ostentatiously taking care of his borrowed horse, feeding it from a bag of carrots he'd had the foresight to bring with him and swearing colourfully at anybody bold enough to hint that he was causing an obstruction.

Kamo felt he was making a fine display of being a cavalry officer. It had been his own idea to attend the robbery in disguise. He'd argued to himself that he was doing it for practical reasons. Wouldn't this identity prove more advantageous than his own? And besides, he simply *enjoyed* dressing up, enjoyed slipping into and out of fictitious lives. But if he were honest, he'd have to admit that his instincts had told him he'd be better not to show his true face, and that the reason for his unusual caution lay with Koba.

His friend's behaviour had been too strange in the preceding days, and indeed ever since he'd returned from that infernal conference. There was the question, for example, of where he intended to be today. First, he'd claimed he would be here with them, despite Kamo's protestations that their chief was too important to place himself in the line of fire. Then he'd spoken vaguely of watching from the rooftops, or a convenient window, or from the courtyard of an adjoining mansion. But Kamo had come to suspect, against his wish to be free of such suspicions, that Koba would be at the train station, where he was easily contactable by his many operatives and could make a swift departure if there was any indication the plan had gone awry.

Was that blameworthy? Absolutely not. Koba was a leader, and a leader was obligated to protect themselves. He would be no use to the Outfit in prison. No, on its own, his caution was commendable. What was it, then, that nagged at Kamo so? There was the unpleasant story he'd heard about Koba being picked up by the Okhrana, a tale he'd found wholly unacceptable—a point he'd made by beating the man who'd divulged it to him until his face was a bloody wreck. In fairness, the gossip might be true. Who hadn't been hauled in at one time or another? Again, on its own, it meant nothing. But why wouldn't Koba have discussed the incident with his lieutenant? Why keep it a secret, unless...?

That was enough of that. In the end, the truth of the matter was that Koba's enthusiasm for this affair had run dry, and it was his, Kamo's fault, for being so half-witted as to nearly blow himself to smithereens weeks before the event. That was why he felt insecure, because his idiocy had almost cost them dearly. Yet that mishap would be behind him after today, Koba would return to how he'd always been, and they'd be heroes to boot, so what benefit was there in worrying? It had never been Kamo's forte. He was infinitely more suited to doing.

And thus far, everything had progressed smoothly. He'd tormented himself over how to camouflage his eyepatch, and whether he could do without it; but dressed as he was, it had become the perfect detail, one last affectation on the part of a vainglorious young soldier who'd probably never fought a battle in his life. Not only would no-one imagine he wasn't what he appeared to be, but he, Patsia, and Anneta had provided an ample diversion for their associates within the tavern and around the square.

The girls had played their roles admirably. Who could distrust a pair of beauties like that, or the dashing officer they chose to lavish their attentions on? They had just as much a taste for drama as he did. And now, having established to those watching that they were empty-headed jezebels with no interest in anything besides finding a well-to-do gentleman, they'd drifted off to assume their positions on either side of the square.

In the meantime, Kamo's performance was nearing its finale. He let his eyes stray to the tavern, where, sure enough, Bachua Kupriashvili was back at his post and ensuring that nobody entered. Instead, he'd be politely suggesting to anyone who wasn't patently a Pharaoh, Cossack, or agent of the Okhrana that they'd do well to avoid Yerevan Square for the foreseeable future.

Elsewhere, others would be spreading a similar

message. They were revolutionaries, not terrorists, and the common folk of Tiflis weren't their target. Better for everyone if the locals could be encouraged to get clear while they were able to. Deciding the time had come to serve his own part toward that end, Kamo picked out two water carriers who'd taken a break and were sitting on their cargo, observing the pageant of the square.

"Hey!" Kamo shouted in their direction. "Be on your way. Haven't you heard? We're sealing this area off. It's official business, so don't make a fuss."

The response he got was a hard stare. Having never been a cavalryman before, Kamo had seemingly overestimated the degree of prestige that came with his uniform.

"Look," he tried again, "there's trouble approaching, and believe me, you're best off out of it."

Maybe the urgency in his voice was more effective than his resort to fake authority had been, because the water carriers grudgingly hoisted up their burdens and ambled onward. However, their attitude made it apparent that clearing the square, or even thinning the crowd, was a bigger task than he'd predicted. After all, the coming and going was endless, and vociferously as the sentries at each street corner were discouraging passersby, there was only so much they could do.

Struck by inspiration, Kamo drew his sabre and waved it around his head. "Get moving, damn you!" he yelled. "The bank carriage will be along at any minute, and if you're too close, you'll be in for it, mark my words."

That got more of a reaction—and some of those reacting would inevitably be the sorts whose curiosity Kamo preferred not to attract. He'd have to hope that his disguise would make them think twice about interfering with him. Nevertheless, though a few of those nearby were shuffling resentfully away, as many had ignored him. And was that really surprising in Tiflis, where resisting authority was a matter of pride?

They were running out of time. Perhaps they already had. Kamo threw caution to the wind: "Do you all want to die?" he bellowed. "If not, get out of here before the bullets start flying!"

In case anyone might have doubted his sincerity, he caught the nearest person by the arm. They happened to be an expensively dressed woman in middle age, whose mouth formed into the roundest O of indignation. Kamo swung her in a half circle and gave her a hearty shove back the way she'd come, and when she looked set to reprimand him, whirled his sabre all the more savagely.

The crowds were definitely diminishing, but still not rapidly enough. And was it his imagination, or did he hear a distant rumble of carriage wheels and many horses? Without warning, Kamo was gripped by a sensation he'd never previously experienced, an agitation that seemed to affect his every nerve. As its initial surge faded, he supposed it could only be panic. His nebulous anxieties of recent weeks had congealed into a single, overwhelming mass, and he knew with visceral certainty that this wasn't going to work. The plan—which was barely worthy of the word!—was flawed in its essentials. Even if they should get the money, they'd never escape with it, and the price of trying would be their lives.

Before he could analyse his inner turmoil further, Kamo was acting on it. To his horse's alarm, he sprang into the saddle and turned its head with a sharp tug of the reins. Then, not daring to consider what he was doing or why, he dug his spurred heels into the animal's flank and set off at breakneck speed out of the square.

TWELVE

Patsia was first to see the convoy.

She'd been hearing it for several seconds by then, over the hubbub of the square and the surrounding streets, as a growing rattle that penetrated to her bones. Or had that been only her excitement? It was as though every cell in her body was tingling. What could be more thrilling than this, than being a bank robber and a revolutionary, and being young, and being here on this perfectly warm day with a gun stowed inside her purse?

There were two carriages. One contained the staff of the bank, as they'd been told to expect: the men in drab suits were an accountant and a cashier. They had four guards with them, and looked cramped and miserable, as anyone might in their circumstances. Patsia felt dimly sorry for them; but then, if they didn't want to robbed, they'd chosen the wrong profession. Anyway, she was more concerned by the second carriage, which was a phaeton and filled to brimming with soldiers, not to mention equipped with a mounted gun. As if guards and soldiers weren't enough, there was also an entourage of stiffly riding Cossacks, two in front, two behind, and one to each side. Put them together and you practically had an army.

Well, Patsia comforted herself, silencing the tremor of fear that danced up her spine, *so do we.*

Even as she finished the thought, she was startled by a conflicting set of hooves. Equally startled were the guards, soldiers, and Cossacks, all of whom became immediately tenser. But unlike Patsia, who was forced to take a hasty step back from the edge of the street, they relaxed when they saw that the disturbance was being caused by a cavalry officer, riding at full pelt and paying them no notice.

That distraction was as good as Patsia was likely to get. Breaking into a run, cursing at the ungainly outfit she'd been obliged to wear, she wondered if the cavalryman was who she supposed he was. She hadn't seen his face, not sufficiently to note whether one eye was hidden by a patch. But if it had been Kamo, what was he doing, riding helter-skelter in the wrong direction? It couldn't be cowardice, Patsia had never met a man more oblivious to its temptations in all of her admittedly brief life. So had the job been called off? Yet Tiflis was positively swarming with youthful cavalry officers, and she'd no means to be sure it was him.

She drove the question from her mind. Even if Kamo had abandoned them, what happened next didn't depend on his presence. In fact, currently it depended on her. She summoned an extra burst of speed, sacrificing any semblance of dignity and hoping that the indecorum of a woman tearing down the street wouldn't alert the convoy that something was amiss.

Her sides were heaving by the time she turned the corner and came within sight of the Pushkin Gardens. She had no breath with which to shout, nor did she believe that shouting, with the leading Cossacks on her heels, would be advisable. Fortunately, Stepko Intskirveli, who waited by the gates there, was looking her way; less fortunately, he seemed to have managed to miss her dashing into view. There were too many people between them, and for a moment she had no idea of what might get his attention.

Frantically she glanced about, conscious of the hoofbeats coming ever closer. She was ready to draw her pistol and start firing into the air if that was what it took, but common sense narrowly restrained her. Then, with a palpable shudder of relief, she recalled the parasol she held tucked under her arm, and which had somehow stayed in place throughout her frenetic dash. Stretched to her full height, Patsia raised it above her head and waved it, as furiously as though it were a semaphore flag and she was on the deck of a sinking ship.

AT THE GATES of the Pushkin Gardens, pushed and shoved and losing what shred of patience he had remaining, Stepko Intskirveli peered across the street, his eyes shuttling to left and right. He thought he could hear horses but wasn't certain. Perhaps it was only the result of being buffeted so, but he was overcome by a conviction that the smallest mistake would bring disaster.

Damn her, where was Patsia? It was exasperating how Kamo put so much faith in those girls of his. And why had no-one apprised him of what she'd be wearing? There were no end of women, many of them adolescent and pretty, and Intskirveli's eyes were blurred with the strain of picking one from another. He longed to check his watch, but that would mean neglecting the street, and what if that should be the decisive juncture? Instead, he lifted a hand to wipe sweat from his brow and held it cupped, squinting against the brightness.

There was a flash of movement. For an instant, he could make no sense of it. Then he interpreted a furled parasol whipping back and forth like an upside-down metronome, and with that, his gaze refocused, and he recognised Patsia, reaching on tiptoes. Now that he saw her, he couldn't imagine how he'd overlooked her.

Intskirveli's heart lurched. "We're off," he muttered, though there was nobody nearby to hear, or nobody he'd want to hear. He swung around giddily, abruptly afraid that it would be he who made the crucial slip, that he'd once more be searching through a sea of bobbing heads, helpless to differentiate them.

But no, there outside the Tilipuchuri tavern was Anneta, and her eyes were fixed on him, as if the world were empty except for the two of them. He had no need of theatrics. Intskirveli simply nodded, and Anneta nodded in return, as if they were twin parts of a mechanism and an electric charge had passed across the intervening distance.

*   *   *

ANNETA HAD BEEN engrossed in guaranteeing that no-one else got into the Tilipuchuri tavern, which was overfull both with revolutionaries and with regular customers, a number of whom were growing restless at the notion of being held prisoner, or perhaps even held hostage. Nobody had explained to them why they weren't being allowed out, since explaining would have been to publicly announce the biggest crime that Tiflis had ever seen.

She couldn't say what had reminded her of her secondary purpose, that of link in a vital chain, but suddenly she was looking to the Pushkin Gardens and straight at Stepko Intskirveli. He was a considerable way away, yet she'd have sworn she could make out the expression in his eyes, which were no more than black specks amid the whiteness of his face. She'd have sworn she'd received his tidings, even before he confirmed them with the tiniest nod of his head.

She returned the nod and stayed like that, head bowed, unable to piece together the import of their exchange. Then her thoughts came unstuck, and she spun toward the entrance of the tavern. *What's the signal?* she asked herself. She racked her brains, until she remembered they'd never agreed on one. But the misgiving was foolish, because everyone was staring at her. She made a beckoning motion, and, in case that was vague, pulled out her Mauser and brandished it.

They'd got the message. The tavern was in an uproar, everybody moving at once, flooding forward, drawing the weapons they'd concealed on their persons or darting for the stashes of bombs and Browning rifles that had been prepared when they'd begun their occupation.

Only in that moment did it occur to Anneta that this was really happening. They were about to shake the city, figuratively and literally. They were going to rob the Tiflis bank, here in plain sight on this sunny day. Probably some of these men and women in front of her would die in the attempt. And in spite of that, or maybe in part because of it, a laugh of pure, ecstatic joy welled up in her chest and found its way to her lips, to pass unnoticed among the general chaos.

Whatever happened, this was going to be glorious.

THIRTEEN

BACHUA KUPRIASHVILI STRODE out through the doorway of the Tilipuchuri tavern, and, having rolled up the newspaper he'd been pretending to read, used it to signal the rest of their band, dispersed around the square. They'd taken no chances; their numbers were swelled by anyone willing to help who could remotely be trusted, making them less of a gang and more a militia.

Kupriashvili let the newspaper drop, content that those who were looking his way would have seen and that those who weren't would have spotted the bank carriage and its retinue, which were already in view. He cocked his pistol, and the noise seemed unnaturally loud.

After all this waiting, everything was happening very quickly. He appraised their forces, and the results were both rousing and disheartening. They were a sorry lot, most of them half-starved from poverty and from devoting so much of themselves to a cause and too little to their own wellbeing. Yet at the same time, that gave them a fearsome energy, an inner heat that glowed in their faces. He'd have sooner been in their company than a thousand of the sort that made up the police, who had full stomachs and no fight in them.

He was their leader for the present, but they didn't need much guidance. Though many weren't Bolsheviks, and there were a few he barely knew to name, they all had their share of experience, be it in the conflict of two years ago or one of the numerous expropriations carried out in recent months. Kupriashvili hurried into the square, not caring who was watching nor disguising the weapon he held. The police weren't trained for an altercation on this scale. They were scarcely trained at all. And they weren't paid enough to warrant placing themselves in the line of fire over other people's money. If they had any sense, they'd be scurrying for cover at the spectacle unfolding before them, twenty well-armed men and women moving as one.

All right, perhaps not quite as one. The truth was that they were more like crabs scattering across a dreary beach than finely honed veterans of the revolutionary war. And Kupriashvili, for all his good intentions, wasn't doing a great deal of leading. He'd rather have yielded that authority to Koba or Kamo, the men who were truly leaders; he'd never had such aspirations. As the convoy bore nearer, he reassured himself that at least theirs was a plan that didn't require an excess of leadership. Setting an example would have to suffice.

He paused in his advance and concentrated instead

on aiming his pistol and taking a shot. He selected the foremost of the Cossacks, since they posed the immediate danger; where everyone else was panicking, they were sizing up targets. They also had the savviness to veer aside, however, and wherever Kupriashvili's shot went, it didn't hit the man he'd picked out.

He had been so focused on the Cossacks that he'd hardly registered the remainder of the convoy behind them. He did so now in broken snatches like reflections in a shattered mirror. He could see that the front carriage was the bank's, and that the driver was urgently turning back the way he'd come. Well, good luck with that! Did he imagine they had nobody posted in that direction? Indeed, all he was doing was impeding the second carriage, the one full of soldiers and furnished with a mounted gun that was the sole genuine threat the defenders possessed. Generally, the soldiers had yet to orient themselves, and those who'd grasped the situation were struggling to put up a resistance that didn't involve inadvertently murdering their allies.

Kupriashvili's band of robbers couldn't afford to be so squeamish. His own first shot had become a volley, as the revolutionaries opened up from every side. It was impossible to judge whether they were achieving anything, but meanwhile, they were getting closer to the carriages, which in turn were fumbling their escape. Hesitant shots were being returned, but Kupriashvili still felt profoundly unworried. Even if the mounted gun on the second carriage should join the fray, it couldn't fire every way simultaneously, and what the soldiers failed to appreciate was that they hadn't been engaged in a gunfight. This sally was only a means for the revolutionaries to bring themselves in range.

Right on cue, the first bomb was thrown. Kupriashvili couldn't identify who by. Could it have been Koba? There'd been rumours he'd be somewhere around, though lately he'd been absent from many of their meetings. At any rate, that the toss fell short of the carriages didn't do much to diminish its effect. The explosion was catastrophic, and in its wake, all Kupriashvili could hear was the tinkling of glass. The shockwave must have blown out the windows encircling the square.

The Cossacks were wheeling their horses, on the verge of disarray, and the soldiers and guards reacted like they'd come under an artillery bombardment, ducking and abandoning all efforts to return fire. Kupriashvili was rocked by a rush of euphoria. They were winning! Against the cohorts of the Tsar, these threadbare revolutionaries with their ill-kept guns and homemade bombs were triumphing! It took the whole of his resolve to remind himself they weren't here to spill the enemy's blood, or to make a statement, or to reignite the dreadful fighting of the abortive insurrection. They were here for one purpose, and that was the money in the lead carriage.

Further bombs flew. If Kupriashvili didn't discern their passage, he assuredly heard them go off. He counted three separate eruptions, each more muffled than the last, drowned out by the increasing ringing in his ears. Through the rising swirls of grey-black smoke, he saw that they'd done what they were intended to. The defenders were in even greater disorder, seeking shelter when there was none to be found, with a mere handful of brave souls making the slightest attempt to fight back. More importantly, one bomb had struck the horses. Their wounds were so hideous that it would have been a mercy if they were dead, and nothing could have driven home to Kupriashvili that this was a day when mercy was vanished from the world as thoroughly as the vision of those desperate beasts endeavouring to break free while their innards slithered from their bellies.

The horses were not the only innocent victims. Bombs might be an effective weapon for a robbery, but they were proving a staggeringly indiscriminate one. All this time, the square had been clearing rapidly, as those stragglers who'd ignored the gang's warnings recognised the cost of their stubbornness. Yet though they'd tried to get to safety, there were many blood-spattered bodies on the ground that didn't belong to either bank guards or Cossacks. The air was choked with screams, human voices competing with the shrieks of equine terror.

But it was becoming harder to fathom the scene through the roiling clouds of smoke that filled the entire centre of the square. And blindness discouraged restraint; several of the robbers were satisfied to lob their bombs and hope for the best. Kupriashvili comprehended with muted horror that this was devolving into a massacre, and that there was nothing to be done about the fact— and worse, that he'd accepted it on some fundamental level, relinquishing any responsibility in the process. The damage was appalling, but all that remained was to ensure this ghastly sacrifice didn't go to waste.

He could just make out the carriages as looming spectres amid the fog. One of them, the larger, was immobile and leaning to the side, its wheels blown off. But the other, to his astonishment, was moving, in a shuddering, jolting fashion. As he watched, it began to pick up speed. The dying horses had decided to express their awful panic with a last bid to flee, and they were prepared to drag the smashed shell of the bank carriage along with them if need be. They couldn't get far, not with such injuries, and yet they were making a respectable pace, and their course would take them through the ring of robbers and out of the square if somebody didn't do something.

So Kupriashvili would do something. Unlike most of his compatriots, he'd kept his bomb in reserve. Now he wrestled it from his pocket and strived to light the fuse with clumsy fingers. By the time he had it burning, the carriage was much nearer and more visible, as its progress sent the smoke heaving away in grey breakers. The tableau was like an episode out of a ghoulish tale told to scare children: the horses were more dead than alive, and still they ran, with a horrid, mechanical motion, crimson froth foaming from their lips.

Kupriashvili tried to remember what Kamo had taught them of the bombs. How long ought he to hold it for? He squinted in fascination at the bright spark that was travelling down toward the metal apple in his palm with a distinctive hiss. He couldn't bring himself to think seriously about hurling the device at those suffering animals. It almost seemed more reasonable that he should hang on to it and see what would happen.

Then reality reasserted itself, and he understood that he'd already left this too late. His throw was dismally inept. In one sense, that didn't matter; he couldn't have missed, with the carriage and the ravaged horses well-nigh upon him. But in another sense, it mattered enormously, because the bomb came to land far too close by him. And Kupriashvili had all of a moment to regret that error before the explosion thrust him off his feet and cast him crashing to the cobbles.

FOURTEEN

DATIKO CHIBRIASHVILI REALISED to his dismay that he was nearest to the carriage—or what was left of the carriage. Kupriashvili had been, but then the idiot had gone and thrown a bomb at short range, which had certainly brought it to a definite halt, but had also sent him flying. Now he lay on the ground, unconscious or perhaps dead.

And that wasn't the half of it. Chibriashvili was standing in a growing pool of slaughtered horse. Kupriashvili's bomb had severed the beasts' legs from their torsos and torn them wide open, and Chibriashvili was getting a lesson on what the interior of a horse looked like that he'd never in his life wished for.

When he took a step toward the carriage, he slopped through blood and worse. He wanted to turn and run, to put as much space between himself and this impromptu abattoir as was humanly possible. But he could dimly descry the carriage's inside, and though the sight was, if anything, more horrible than that outside—there was absolutely no doubt the passengers were dead—he could also see two bulky bags.

Chibriashvili had no desire to do what he did next, but there wasn't anybody else. He reached into the carriage, ignoring the flagrant stench of offal, and grabbed the bags, one in each hand.

Before he had them out, he'd come to a crucial understanding: the bags were too damned heavy. How could it be that no-one had considered this detail? It was utterly ridiculous. All the planning that had gone into attaining this prize, and nobody had taken into account that lifting two bags laden with money was akin to hoisting leaden weights. Then again, maybe the idea had been that they'd commandeer the carriage itself, in which case, shouldn't the point have been made that bombs weren't an ideal weapon?

He looked for someone to aid him. There was no establishing which of the ghostly forms shambling through the murk were on his side. He thought about crying out, but in this darkness, a Cossack might be beside him and he'd never notice. However, the alternative was to creep onward at a snail's pace, and probably to be caught by the multitudes of police that must inevitably be on their way.

He paused, having covered barely any distance, to ponder whether there wasn't some more efficient method by which to carry the bags. If he bundled them in his arms, might he be able to stagger along like that? A rebellious part of his mind asked whether he wouldn't be best to get away with one of them, rather than be caught red-handed with both. Could he be blamed? For that matter, if he ripped open a bag and stuffed notes into his pockets, if he filled his shirt with them and ran, wouldn't that be better than nothing?

He had nearly talked himself into it when he heard the sound of hooves and clattering wheels. They couldn't represent either of the two carriages, those weren't going anywhere. Though the haze that still hung over the square distorted noise as it did everything, he was confident the sound was approaching from one of the incoming roads. There was no way that boded well, yet Chibriashvili was frozen by indecision. What if someone had observed him getting the money out? What if someone was observing him now? There was an eeriness and an untrustworthiness to the cascading smoke; for an instant, he'd be capable of seeing quite clearly, and then the next he'd be blind. He could readily believe that half the gang might be near, wondering what he'd do.

The hooves, the wheels, were already close. There was no prospect of his getting away with the money. The question was whether he dared to leave it—and the answer was that he didn't. Arrest frightened him, as did the likelihood of being shot by an enthusiastic Pharaoh or soldier, but neither frightened him as much as Koba and Kamo. Kamo especially; Chibriashvili had witnessed enough of the man's passion for violence to know what would be in store for him if he should go back and explain that he'd abandoned the money to save his skin.

So he stood there imbecilically, the bags at his feet, as the vehicle finished its phantasmal approach, the smoke parting only at the last to reveal it. Chibriashvili debated raising his hands and didn't. He gazed as though hypnotised, watching the carriage manoeuvre like a bear lumbering in a snowstorm.

It was a phaeton, and the driver was its lone passenger. He was dressed in a rather ill-fitting uniform and a skewed eyepatch. He appeared to be a cavalryman, but that didn't account for his presence. Was he some preposterous heroic type who'd elected to take matters upon himself? Except, something about him was curiously familiar.

The driver's one visible eye roved across Chibriashvili's face and then down to the two bags lying on the cobbles. He grinned a lascivious grin, and, to Chibriashvili's immense shock, called, "Ho, Chibriashvili! Hurry up, damn you!"

It took an inordinate effort for Chibriashvili to stop his jaw from hanging. But having closed his mouth, he realised he'd have to open it again to speak. "Kamo... is that you?"

"Who else? Get a move on, you bloody fool."

Chibriashvili could make no sense of the situation. He lifted one of the bags and reeled, having forgotten how much they weighed. The bag slipped from his fingers and he contemplated its fall with dread, to feel intense relief as it refrained from bursting on impact. He knelt and tugged at it once more, but it seemed that his body was no longer accurately receiving the commands his brain was giving. A dreamy quality had pervaded everything and he was helpless to defy it.

"Cretin!"

The word was followed by a cuff to the rear of his head, and he looked up into a pretty, exultant face smeared with soot and dirt. She, too, was someone he knew: Alexandra, one of the young women that apparently served as Kamo's personal escort. She was carrying a rifle, the barrel of which currently rested lazily on her shoulder. Without lowering it, she seized the bag he'd been grappling with in her free hand, let out a grunt of annoyance as she discovered its heaviness, and hauled it onto the seat of the phaeton.

Chibriashvili's cheeks were fiery with shame. Determinedly he gripped the other bag, not trying to emulate her, only to get it off the ground, and this time he succeeded in cradling it in his arms and lurching over to the carriage. Gasping, he all but dropped it in Kamo's lap, managing in the end to ensure that it slid instead into the footwell. He stumbled back, eager to be elsewhere.

Alexandra, by contrast, was halfway to clambering up into the seat beside Kamo before he waved her roughly away. That done, he brought the phaeton around in an awkward arc and hurtled off, as Chibriashvili gaped after him, not quite willing to accept the evidence of his own eyes.

FIFTEEN

KAMO CROSSED THE perimeter of the square and started into the street beyond, still unable to believe that his scheme had worked. He had ridden about in something like a panic, conscious every moment that, by chasing after a solution to a possibly imaginary problem, he might have sabotaged the robbery in its entirety. Yet his instincts had insisted with such adamantine surety that this was what he ought to do: that his choice was to take this risk or to guarantee failure.

So he'd searched frenziedly through the streets of Tiflis for the resource he was convinced he needed, and had continued his search even when an explosion announced that the expropriation had begun. And just as he was losing hope, he'd come across what he sought.

Unsurprisingly, the phaeton's owners hadn't been thrilled to surrender it. But Kamo had explained emphatically that the fate of the city, and indeed the fate of the Georgian nation, hung in the balance, which was so close to the truth that he'd hardly considered it a deception. Mind you, he'd also promised to return the carriage when he was done, and that was most definitely a lie. This vehicle would be a burning wreck somewhere on the outskirts of town by nightfall.

At any rate, Kamo's decision had been the right one, and the proof was that here he was, escaping with a fortune in roubles, a bounty that would make every other revolutionary bank robber in the world despair. Let Koba doubt him now; let anyone suggest that the mere matter of nearly losing an eye would hold back Kamo, bandit extraordinaire!

Or so he thought, until he turned the next corner and saw the second carriage that was rapidly advancing on him, crammed full of policemen.

One of their number stood out particularly, distinguished by his elaborate uniform and by his manner. All of them seemed nervous, as anybody would who was hurrying toward rather than away from a string of explosions, but this one figure evidently bore a greater burden of worry, which he was ineffectually concealing behind a veneer of stolid nobility.

Kamo recognised the man. His name was Balabanksy and he was the deputy police chief. Moreover, the two of them were looking straight at each other; Kamo had been staring all this while, and Balabanksy, perhaps sensing his scrutiny, had begun staring back.

Kamo was struck by the absurdity of his plight and most of all by its unfairness. He'd won, hadn't he? Wasn't it an outrageously cruel coincidence that these Pharoahs should happen to be approaching by the road on which he was making his escape? They were practically beside him now, close enough that he and Balabanksy could have reached out and touched hands.

It occurred to Kamo that he would have to say something. It was that or stop and give himself up—or else open fire and make a break for it. Actually, that third possibility was the most appealing, and he'd never have a better opportunity to assassinate a deputy police chief than this. Wisdom prevailed; a solitary man against half a dozen was bad odds. No, his talent for dissimulation had served him well today, and mightn't he pull off one more impossible stunt?

But he hadn't a clue what words were appropriate for such circumstances. "The money's safe," he babbled in desperation. "Run to the square." It was farcical. How could they not find it suspicious that a cavalry officer was riding alone in a carriage in the opposite direction, and, having become suspicious, not remark that next to him were two overstuffed bags? And why had he said *run*? He almost wanted to apologise for his asininity, to hand over his loot like an embarrassed schoolchild with a pocketful of pilfered sweets.

Except that the other carriage wasn't slowing. And while Balabanksy was still looking at him, it wasn't with suspicion but with the boggle-eyed distraction of a man whose job had been to prevent precisely the sort of debacle that awaited him ahead. Here was someone with no recourse and no excuses, who'd failed to avert a crime that had been the talk of the town for months, and he might have been driving to the gallows. The last thing he cared about was some idiotic cavalry officer keen to save his own neck.

Kamo felt a glimmer of pity for Balabanksy, and an equal compulsion to laugh at him, and instead concentrated on keeping his features a perfectly blank mask for the remaining instant. Then Balabanksy was gone, reduced to a dwindling clack of hooves, and Kamo knew that there was nobody in the whole of Tiflis who could stop him, because he'd just driven past the deputy police chief and had done so without an iota of trouble.

He carried on in rather a daze. This setting didn't seem altogether real. It was as if the reality was the madness behind him and this relative peace and quiet was an illusion. But for all that, the robbery had left its mark. So far from the square, windows were cracked and shattered, as though the locals had spent the morning fighting with thrown stones. People peeked out at him as he passed, and the more courageous were in the streets, gawking toward the square and theorising in loud whispers. What would they think if they were aware of what had happened, and that the proceeds had been borne past their very noses? But none of them heeded him, even less so than Balabanksy had.

The rest of his trip was easy going, which was a good thing given that Kamo was barely functioning. The only manoeuvre that required much in the way of attention was when he turned off Vtoraya Goncharnaya Street and into the yard of the joiner's shop there, which was owned by one Babe Bochoridze, affiliate to the Bolshevik cause.

Babe wasn't out waiting as he'd expected her to be,

but obviously she'd been listening for signs of an arrival, because the old woman emerged immediately and bustled to meet him, her face betraying how dubious she'd been that anyone would make this rendezvous. She had the sense not to ask him questions, though her eyes widened when she saw the bags.

Kamo climbed from the seat. His mind was still working sluggishly. He peered down at himself, and was puzzled for a moment by the uniform he wore. It wouldn't take a great deal of ingenuity to put two and two together, or to establish that the cavalry officer who'd been showing off before the robbery and the one who'd ridden away at high speed and the one who'd raced by the deputy police chief in a stolen phaeton were all the same man. More even than the carriage and the bags, his costume was a sure giveaway.

"I'll need a change of clothes," he mumbled.

He stood there swaying. He knew he should be carrying the money inside, but he had neither the stamina nor the inclination. And the wait for Babe to return seemed very long, far longer that it could be. By the time she appeared again, he wondered if perhaps he'd fallen asleep on his feet, and yet he wasn't refreshed in the slightest.

The clothes she'd brought him were a plain shirt and trousers. Babe looked faintly startled when Kamo began to undress right there in the yard, without checking to see if he was being observed. The buttons of his jacket were stiff and unwieldy, and he had to resist an itch to tear them off. He grew angry, but the anger was distant, like a storm viewed from indoors. When at last he'd managed to strip and was pulling on the fresh clothing, he felt liberated, as if it were a constricting skin he'd shed.

However, the simple process of changing clothes had drained whatever remaining resources he possessed. Kamo staggered with an exhaustion he hadn't fully realised he was enduring. He really thought he'd collapse. Glancing around for something against which to steady himself, he found that he was gazing, instead, at a brimming pail of water. With the dregs of his fading strength, Kamo picked up the bucket and tipped it over his head, gasping at the coldness.

The water was a marvel, restoring him utterly. He stood shivering and trying not to laugh amid a spreading puddle. He gave his head a ferocious canine shake and watched the drops spatter. And only then did he notice how Babe was staring at him, half in amusement and half in terror.

He grabbed one of the two bags. It hardly seemed to weigh anything at all. Hoisting it onto a shoulder, he pointed to the other. "Stop gawping, Babe, and get that, will you?"

Without delaying for a reply, Kamo marched off to begin the business of stashing his magnificently ill-gotten gains.

SIXTEEN

HE COULDN'T RESTRAIN himself. Eliso Lominadze had to go back and look.

It was a mad impulse, he had no illusions on that score. Few deeds were stupider than returning to the scene of a crime, and absolutely nothing could be stupider than returning to the scene of such a crime as this, which had combined all the worst extremes of robbery, vandalism, murder, and terrorism.

Then again, it was that which made Lominadze so abundantly certain he had to obey this urge. What they'd committed was simply too big. He wasn't ready to put it behind him. He was in no state to interpret the confusion of emotions he was feeling, or the million thoughts battering around his mind, but he did know that if he was to get through this day, the first crucial step would be to see with clear eyes what it was he'd done. He had flashes of memories that declined to fit together. He'd thrown a bomb; at what? He'd fired off numerous rounds; at whom, and had any of them found their target? Should he be proud? Should he feel guilty? It was terrible to have this vast pressure of emotion and not be able to shape it into a meaningful form.

All right, so he was being irrational. He'd admitted as much, even as he'd formulated ever more nonsensical rationalisations. And the only reassurance he had was that he hadn't completely taken leave of his senses. He'd made time to disguise himself before he started back.

Of course, it might be argued that stealing a disguise on the day you went to gape at the results of a robbery you'd been a part of minutes prior wasn't entirely sensible either. And in the world of subterfuge, he doubted a teacher's uniform would be highly regarded. But he'd seen that a teachers' conference was occurring and some perverseness had been enough to send him rushing inside to snatch a new outfit, and then scuttling into an alley, where he'd pulled it on over his own smoke-stained, stinking clothes. Fortunately, the uniform was considerably too large for him, but the inverse was that he now resembled a teacher who couldn't buy clothes that fit.

Altogether, Lominadze would have been forced to concede that what he was doing went beyond mere stupidity into some heady realm of idiocy he had no name for. Yet as he came to the border of the square, his steps increasingly halting, he understood that he needn't have worried about anybody noting the eccentricities of his clothing. He might as well have been a ghost, and were that so, he'd have been another among many.

To say that Erivansky Square looked as if a battle had raged there was somehow inadequate. This was worse than a battlefield, worse because its basis was normality, even gaiety. A substantial number of the casualties had been out enjoying the fine weather before they'd found themselves trapped on the front line of a minor war. Thus, though the overwhelming colour of the square was red, there were incongruent patches of other bright shades, vibrant blues and yellows and purples and greens. In one place, an open parasol floated; at another, a canvas bag had been dropped and spewed its contents, which sat like islands in a crimson lake. It was incredible that so much blood could have been spilled, incredible to think that anyone might have survived such an astronomical act of violence.

But people had. Those of the wounded who could move were making their way by agonising stages toward the edges of the square, perhaps gripped by the delirious fear that the robbers might return for a reprise at any moment. Those who couldn't move lay panting or sobbing or mouthing noiselessly. Many of them would be dead by nightfall, Lominadze could tell as much at a glance. And nobody was making an effort to help them, or doing anything whatsoever. A mood of paralysis hung, as though the gunpowder odour that still laced the air was a numbing miasma.

Lominadze had seen all he wanted to see. Indeed, he suspected he would keep on seeing this in his dreams for days or weeks or months to come, that as an old man he'd refuse to recount the tale of the great Tiflis bank heist lest the image should bubble up afresh in his memory. As he turned and stumbled away, he was already trying his hardest to forget.

PART THREE

SEVENTEEN

THE TIFLIS THAT Maro Bochoridze and her husband Mikha drove their small cart through was a changed city. There was no comfort in knowing that they were the ones who'd changed it, not when they were out amid the legacy of what they'd done.

Maro had been aware that the robbery, if they should by some miracle pull it off, would stir things up. Her imagination hadn't been equal to the task of conceiving what that would truly mean. She'd pictured more police, or burly Cossacks making a show of their presence. But this? She felt that the months had been rolled back, plunging them into the harsh reprisals of the year before last. From the authorities' perspective, it seemed that a successful bank robbery was very much on a par with a failed revolution.

So yes, the police were mobilised, every one of them.

But the army had been deployed also, and in extravagant numbers. Everywhere roads had been closed, often without apparent logic, and Erivansky Square was shut off so thoroughly it could have vanished from the city. What they hoped to accomplish was anyone's guess. Did they suppose the money might have slipped between the cobbles somewhere? If the rumours of a special detective unit having been formed were true, perhaps they believed they could compile from bloody footprints and spent bullet casings and the bewildered, contradictory accounts of eyewitnesses a comprehensive portrait that would lead them to the perpetrators.

Maro wasn't afraid on that count. The robbery was one gigantic red herring, with practically every revolutionary in Tiflis involved to a greater or lesser extent. The authorities could chase loose ends for a year and still not find their way back to Koba and Kamo. After all, no-one was quite certain where Koba had been—though there were competing stories placing him at various points within a wide radius of the square—and Kamo had worn his ludicrous disguise the whole time, unbeknownst to everyone except Anneta, Patsia, and Alexandra.

However, there was no real need to identify ringleaders when the Okhrana knew most of the Tiflis revolutionaries by name, address, and a dozen other details, and when they could progress via hunches and the kicking in of doors. Eventually one of those doors would belong to Maro and her husband, likely sooner rather than later, and that was why they were here now, much as she'd have preferred to be enjoying the relative and probably false safety of staying inside.

The cart was achingly slow, in part due to its heavy cargo and in part due to the age and unwillingness of the nag pulling them, and it was that bit more infuriating to admit that they couldn't have hurried even had they wanted to, since hurrying would have looked suspicious. Obviously, that they were here at all looked suspicious, but there were degrees; life in Tiflis couldn't simply stop just because tens of people had died, hundreds of thousands of roubles had been stolen, and innumerable windows had been shattered by explosions. There were markedly less folks around, but they'd passed a few vehicles since they'd set out, and Maro told herself that there was no reason for them to attract attention. She and Mikha were two perfectly normal locals, on an errand important enough to warrant braving a city on lockdown.

Their route had been far from the quickest, as a series of diversions had nudged them from the straightest path, some planned—they definitely didn't intend to go anywhere near the square—and some not. Presently they were approaching another junction, and Maro's gaze was drawn to a diminutive figure on the corner: a ragged girl with dirt caked into her hair and skin and patched clothing, and a gleam in her eyes that was a compromise between wildness and shy subservience. As Maro spied her, the girl made a gesture with her hands, which were crossed over her scrawny stomach. She extended the left like a bird's wing and kept the right as it was, fingers pointed downward. Then she grinned the most disarming grin Maro had seen.

Mikha, too intent on driving, hadn't been watching,

and they were nearly at the junction, and so Maro dug an elbow into his ribs. To his credit, Mikha didn't flinch, only turned them with a yank of the reins. There was a Pharaoh in spitting distance of the girl, but the entire transaction had been carried off so smoothly that he hadn't paid a hint of notice to either her or them.

The girl was one of the mob of urchins Koba had somehow recruited, and who were fiercely loyal to him for reasons nobody seemed terribly sure of. They were out in force today, on his orders, scattered among the streets, there to provide guidance as the girl had. They could move freely and not receive a second look, because what were the chances of traversing a Tiflis street without encountering at least one ragamuffin? And they'd been doing admirably. Maro could readily imagine them spread across the city, scampering through alleys and relaying messages and constructing their own constantly updating map of their opponents' positions.

The road they'd swerved into was a winding concourse bordered by crumbling apartment houses. Halfway along its length, a scruffy creature appeared from nowhere and ran in front of them. Was that a signal? By the time Maro had thought to hunt for an additional clue, they'd melted into the shadows of a doorway. But Mikha evidently believed so. Arriving at a crossroads, he steered them right, though it would protract their journey yet again.

They continued for a minute at the same torturous rate, passing turn-offs without any tattered youths materialising to suggest that they do otherwise. Maro was beginning to feel a stirring of optimism. Even if they were travelling by the longest, most tangled route, they weren't far from their destination, and they'd met with no serious difficulties.

The reflection had scarcely crossed her mind before a child was dashing into the street ahead of them. It was a boy, with a rat's nest of black hair and a pale, pockmarked face marred further by a jagged scar down his cheek. As he sprinted by, he proceeded to flap his skinny arms frantically above his head, in spite of the policemen posted here as everywhere. The boy didn't look at Maro or Mikha or at the carriage, and did a fair job of selling his display as some random burst of juvenile excitement. Yet it was transparently meant for them, and he kept it up until he was on the opposite pavement. Clearly, he was indicating that they were going the wrong way.

But they couldn't turn around, the boy himself had seen to that. There were two policemen regarding them, and doing so would have been blatant. Their sole alternative was to trundle on, toward whatever doom awaited them.

As they rounded the following bend, that doom transpired to be a roadblock, consisting of a wooden barricade and four soldiers. The barricade was hastily built and the soldiers evinced the bored irritability of functionaries who considered their duty a tremendous waste of time, and still Mikha had no choice except to bring the cart to a halt in the gap that had been left vacant.

The soldiers didn't seem especially concerned. A couple of them, who were chatting and smoking cigarettes, didn't bother themselves to look up. If Maro and Mikha had been armed, they could perhaps have fought their way through, though today of all days, a gunshot would have drawn armed men like wasps to a wedding banquet.

The soldier who did respond was the youngest, probably not even twenty. He trudged over to them with the glazed weariness of someone who'd been on his feet for too many hours already, and, on reaching them, said, "I'm going to inspect your cargo," in a manner that managed to be at once matter-of-fact and apologetic.

"Of course," Mikha agreed. Maro felt he did well not to append the customary declaration of guilty people everywhere, *We've got nothing to hide.*

The soldier walked around to the back of the cart. He kept darting nervous glances at his comrades in the hope that one of them would think to cover him. But none of them were showing much interest. When he got to the tailboard, he let it down with care, using his left hand only so that he didn't have to surrender his rifle. With that done, he stared at the tarpaulin thus revealed as if it were a pit he was preparing to leap into.

All of this Maro watched by craning in her seat until she was twisted almost double. She didn't dare to dismount. She'd thought the young soldier might summon her or Mikha, but he hadn't, and she couldn't persuade herself that it would be right to volunteer.

Fortunately, the soldier mustered the requisite courage. This time, he did abandon his rifle, propping it against the flank of the cart, near enough that he could grab it if their cargo should turn out to be one of violent revolutionaries or bundled banknotes. He gripped the tarpaulin with both hands and tugged it over. Then he peered at the object he'd unveiled, which, folded in two, filled the space of the cart.

"It's a mattress," Maro said helpfully.

The soldier scowled. "I can see that. But what are you doing with it?"

"We're taking it to the observatory," Mikha contributed.

"The observatory?" the soldier replied, as though he didn't know what such a thing was.

"To the Tiflis Meteorological Observatory," Maro clarified.

"It's to go on the couch there," Mikha explained.

The soldier didn't appear to find this a very compelling justification. For a dreadful moment, Maro was convinced he was about to test the mattress by jabbing the bayonet of his rifle into it. He tilted the weapon experimentally and the resolve was written across his face.

Even as Maro held her breath, the soldier presumably realised that a mattress would be of little use to anyone with a gash cut in it and that his remit didn't extend to wanton vandalism. He lowered the rifle, freed a hand, and settled for giving the fabric a hard prod. Maro didn't release the breath. What result did he expect? Was he merely being thorough, or had he decided that no honest person would regard mattress-moving as a vital errand the day after the biggest robbery in the city's history? If there'd been a scrap of air in her lungs, Maro might have cursed him out loud, because his expression was inscrutable, and she couldn't judge whether that was due to canniness or stupidity.

"And you say you're taking this to the observatory?" the soldier asked.

Oh, thank goodness, it was stupidity. "Yes. To go

on the couch." With imbecilic innocence to match the soldier's own, Maro added, "We didn't know there'd be all this fuss."

"There was a robbery. But nobody's told us to look out for mattresses."

Wanting badly to laugh, she wrangled her features into an arrangement that she hoped spoke of mild puzzlement. "A robbery? We'd have put this off if we'd known, I'm sure they could have waited."

"That might have been best," the soldier concurred. "But you're here now, eh?" And with a perilous wave of his rifle, he motioned for them to be on their way.

Mikha obeyed his instruction, and it impressed Maro that he got the horse moving and the cart rattling onward again without undue haste. Soon they were past the next corner, the barricade behind them, the road ahead clear of obstruction, and their destination only three more streets away, and Maro could have sobbed with relief, or as easily guffawed at how absurd this all was. A day ago, she could never have imagined herself so invested in the fate of a mattress.

Once they had the money, their dilemma had become what to do with it. Where, in a city on furious alert, could it possibly be safe? It was Koba who'd come up with the solution, and, for all that Maro had secretly never much liked the man, she had to admit his idea was ingenious. She'd been astonished to learn that he had once been employed, briefly, at the local observatory, and that he was still in contact with the staff there, enough that a gift wouldn't seem altogether strange. And since it would need to be something large, what could be better than a new mattress to replace the threadbare one they'd been tolerating for years?

So it was that she and Babe Bochoridze had been up all night, working in shifts to sew banknotes into the interior of a freshly purchased mattress in such a fashion that their presence would pass a casual inspection. And so it was that, by the end of the day, the head of the observatory would be seated on top of 341,000 roubles and no-one would be any the wiser.

EIGHTEEN

KOBA HAD KNOWN they'd come for him. The only question had been when.

No, that wasn't quite true, he thought, as he opened the door in response to the savage hammering on its other side. There was also the question of how far they intended to go. One of the Okhrana's many eccentricities was that, in their own unfathomable way, they tended to play more or less fair. They might bully, blackmail, fake evidence and falsify testimony, might arrange the most disproportionate punishments for petty offences and turn a blind eye to anything up to murder if they believed a bigger fish could be snared by doing so; but essentially they focused their attentions on those they perceived to be legitimately guilty and kept the innocent out of it.

But now they'd come to his home, rather than adopting a modicum of discretion. Clearly, all bets were off.

There were four of them, they were stout men, and it didn't take the bulges in their jackets to inform him they were armed. For an instant, Koba was genuinely alarmed. Would they push their way inside? Would they drag Kato and little Iakob into this? Kato was already shaken, since their apartment was close to the square and she'd heard the explosions at first hand. Traditionally the Okhrana showed restraint when it came to families, but again, it was evident the robbery had consigned such traditions to the past.

Thankfully, they made no attempt to enter. The man in the lead, the least thuggish of the lot, pronounced, "Joseph Djugashvili? You're coming with us."

So, they didn't aim to search the apartment. That could mean any number of things, none of which were unequivocally good. "Let me get my hat and coat," Koba said.

He'd half expected an argument. Instead, the four watched him like hawks from where they stood. As he pulled on his coat, Koba caught Kato's eye. She was in the doorway to the apartment's second room, hidden from the entrance, with Iakob cradled in her arms. Her bearing was one of dogged determination, and Koba experienced an enormous surge of pride. He'd married a brave woman, a woman fit to be the wife of a revolutionary.

But he said nothing, didn't so much as acknowledge her. He strode to the outer door and kept going, leaving the four men no option except to be collided with or to part. It took them only a moment to gather their wits, and for two of them to dart in front of him, trapping him in their midst, but still Koba felt he'd achieved a minor victory.

As before, there was a carriage ready. Unlike the other, this wasn't open, and a pang of trepidation afflicted him as he clambered in, as though he were stepping voluntarily into a cage. Yet all that happened was that the four agents got in after him, one sitting to either side and the remaining pair opposite, so that they could peer at him with overt hostility throughout the journey.

They seemed to be travelling for a long time, and Koba gave up keeping track of the twists and turns. Plausibly their sole purpose was to disorient him and let the menace of his circumstances sink in. He feigned indifference, and after a while closed his eyes. Maybe there was no feigning about it; he really couldn't bring himself to be concerned. He thought he might even have gone to sleep if it weren't for the carriage's vibration.

The fact was that they'd won, that *he* had won. The money was theirs and soon would be Lenin's, once they'd concocted a method to transfer it out of the country. These things he believed with imperturbable faith, as if they'd already happened. He had secured his position in the upper echelons of the Bolsheviks, and nothing these men did to him would impede his destiny. Lock him up and he'd escape. Exile him to Siberia and he'd find a way back. And if they chose to execute him? Well, perhaps he'd find his way back from that, too.

When they eventually stopped, it was again in a residential area, giving the forceful impression that this might not be real, but a recurring vision that would haunt him indefinitely: every few weeks, phantoms would come and haul him off on a trip such as this, to a building such as this, to an encounter such as that which lay within. And likely there was an element of truth to that, if he should stay in Tiflis, and if he should somehow get through the next minutes.

They led him upstairs, to a landing and a particular door. He got the sense that they owned the entire building, and the stairs had been scuffed with the marks of regular passage. This place was more upmarket than the last, and Koba wondered if there was any significance to that. Had he graduated to some higher level of official interest? Certainly, the apartment beyond the door was positively dignified. Yet a glance around confirmed that nobody lived there, or not permanently. It had the air of a façade, and only compounded his feeling of being caught in something illusory.

The setting was comfortable, not like an interrogation room at all. There were stuffed chairs and even a sideboard. The man who sat waiting, however, didn't look the least bit at ease. As Koba had been ushered inside, he'd reacted with a twitch of his whole body, as though he wished to get up and kept himself from doing so by an act of intense willpower. Koba recognised Mukhtarov from their previous interview, and the Okhrana officer was distinctly the worse for wear.

Was he supposed to sit? Koba liked the notion of standing better, and no-one was giving him an indication either way. As a compromise, he paced farther into the room. The agents who'd brought him made no move to follow, and he stopped when he was well clear of them. There was a large double window, and it struck him that, in a pinch, he might be able to fling himself through it. Granted they were on the third floor, but it might still be preferable to what they had in mind.

"I imagine you're aware of why you're here," Mukhtarov said. The tension in his posture was there in his voice also.

"I've no idea," Koba replied, quite honestly. No need to add that he could think of several possibilities.

Mukhtarov's attitude was unsympathetic. "Yes, you do. You were seen watching Erivansky Square when the robbery occurred. Will you deny it?"

Koba didn't, but he did shrug, as though the question were a trivial one. "I was nearby. So were a lot of people. And who wasn't watching? There were explosions, obviously I was curious as to what was going on."

Mukhtarov's eyes narrowed. "You knew precisely what was going on."

"Oh, I knew it must be the robbery," Koba confessed blithely. "But who'd have guessed they'd make such a show of it? So, yes, I hung around for a minute to watch, before the bullets really started flying. Is that a crime?"

"It is," Mukhtarov said, "if we decide that it is."

Koba had no retort. Mukhtarov was right; if the Okhrana chiefs felt they'd save themselves best by punishing everyone they suspected of being remotely connected to the robbery, then they'd do so without hesitation.

"And this man," Mukhtarov said, "the one you referred to when last we met as *Kamo*... Ter-Petrosian, that's his real name, isn't it? The description you gave us must have been false, or else he wasn't leading the attack. Nobody was identified by any of the witnesses who matched that depiction."

Koba had to stifle a smile. How could he have predicted that Kamo would attend in a borrowed costume? The lunatic was a law unto himself. Koba spread his hands in a gesture that asked, *And what am I to do about that?* "I've never met him. How could I describe him perfectly? They say he's a master of disguise, so probably he was in disguise when he led the robbery. But if you have his name, why can't you track him down?"

The answer was that Kamo was in hiding and would remain that way until the heat had subsided enough that he could flee the city. Koba didn't know where he currently was and wouldn't have revealed the information if he had. There'd been a time, not so long ago, when he'd been willing to sacrifice the Outfit's unreliable and hazardously insane leader, trusting that his captors wouldn't get anything out of him and might conceivably relax their efforts in the belief they had the ringleader in custody. Yet Kamo had, against all odds, not only led the Outfit to success but played a crucial part, and that earned a degree of loyalty, in the short term anyway.

Mukhtarov, though, wasn't done. "I think you know more than you're letting on," he said. "We've evidence that the two of you have been seen together. Why shouldn't we suppose that you deliberately misled us?"

"Why should you? I realised when you last dragged me in that if I didn't help you, I'd end up in trouble. So I spilled my guts, and it's unlucky for us both that there wasn't much of value to be found there."

"Not much?" Mukhtarov snapped. "There was

nothing! Nothing you told us was the slightest use. Even the location you gave was wrong. We wasted men on your word."

"Truthfully, I'm at a loss as to what you want from me. If you wasted men on my word, you ought to have listened when I told you my word was no good."

Koba hadn't meant to sound quite so exasperated or contemptuous as he had, but still he was taken aback when Mukhtarov jolted from his chair and lurched toward him, face crimson, with a garbled cry of, "You rotten bastard!"

Then Mukhtarov's fist was pounding into Koba's jaw. Mukhtarov was strong for a man of his age, and he'd had surprise on his side. While there was no doubt that Koba could have handled his adversary in a straight fight, the blow sent him reeling, and by then the Okhrana officer was on him, planting a couple of clumsy kicks before wading in with his fists. Even so, Koba could have defended himself, and done more, as well; since they hadn't bothered to search him, he had a small and viciously sharp knife tucked into the back of his trousers. But he promptly resolved that he was best off letting this run its course, so long as he was never in true danger.

He wasn't. Though Mukhtarov's initial punch had been solid enough, after that he was basically flailing, and in any case, his associates wouldn't allow him to keep this up forever. Koba struggled to observe what was happening, with his arms wrapped around his head and one bruised eye squeezed shut, but he still enjoyed the sight of four junior Okhrana agents endeavouring to restrain their superior without appearing to, and it only improved as it became obvious that Mukhtarov had no intention of being so easily rebuffed.

They hadn't expected this and hadn't a clue what to do. Koba could see the mounting dismay in their faces, replacing all their studied confidence. And with that knowledge, he understood that he'd walk out of here— that, ultimately, he'd triumphed. Mukhtarov had gone off script, and whatever ending the Okhrana had written for this play, whatever Koba's preordained role had been, it would never come to pass.

The fight went out of Mukhtarov with startling suddenness, as if he'd reached the same conclusion. Viewed calmly, Koba's involvement might have been all too manifest, but calm was a privilege nobody could afford just now, and so Mukhtarov had snatched up his suspect prematurely and asked the wrong questions and finally had thrown away his authority altogether, with his own men as much as with Koba.

Koba got to his feet and batted dirt from his jacket. He sought to look hurt, emotionally as well as physically. "There was no call for that," he mumbled, wiping a trickle of blood from his split bottom lip.

"Shut your mouth," Mukhtarov demanded, rather weakly. He seemed feeble and deflated.

"Absolutely." Koba refused to be denied the last word.

Mukhtarov could have regained the initiative if he'd tried, but his eyes were glassy and his cheeks were fiercely red and he'd apparently lost all interest in the situation. A few seconds went by, and one of the lackeys who'd brought Koba took it on himself to put an end to this farrago.

"Come on," he said to Koba. "We're finished with you for the moment. But we'll be watching, do you hear? You'll be seeing us again, and soon. So, if you truly don't know anything, you'd better start learning what you can, because next time we won't be this gentle."

Koba didn't look at Mukhtarov, his defeated enemy, as they escorted him out the door. He maintained his hurt expression as they descended the stairs, but couldn't keep a spring from his step. He was over the final hurdle. More than that, he beheld his future clearly. The night had confirmed what he'd already surmised: he and Tiflis were done with each other.

It was time to leave, and time to sever certain ties, at least for the present. The Outfit was too hot to handle and so was the money it had acquired with such unforeseen efficiency. Henceforward, both would be Kamo's problem.

NINETEEN

THERE WERE WORSE duties than being on guard at the train station. Tugushi knew so, having been assigned to many of them in recent days.

The problem, in essence, was the scope of the brief handed down to them. Had they been told, "Find the bank robbers," then that was a task with its own reasonable limits and a definite outcome. Oh, not an outcome they were ever likely to reach; the combined forces of the police and army, with the interference of the Okhrana and that accursed, self-satisfied special detective unit, had failed to turn up a single perpetrator, or at any rate a single person they could categorically pin anything on. Still, "find the bank robbers" was a job description you could get behind.

Unfortunately, that wasn't their brief. Indeed, Tugushi would have been challenged to define exactly what their orders were, but if he'd had to put them into words, the result would have been along the lines of "Shake down the revolutionary underground of Tiflis and see what falls out, and if it should happen to have something to do with the robbery that made us all look like imbeciles and drove the deputy police chief to suicide, make damn sure you follow that lead into the very bowels of hell if you have to."

Which was understandable if you didn't know Tiflis, as the special detective unit evidently didn't and as the local Okhrana officials sometimes gave the impression of not doing. Because the revolutionary underground of this city was virtually every street, cellar, corner, and attic. Tiflis had revolutionaries the way dogs had fleas, and you couldn't assume they were confined to the lower tiers of society, either. Many a fashionable noble or wealthy business owner felt justified in throwing their riches at a Bolshevik here or a Menshevik there. What were they to do, lock up every third man and woman?

Why, plainly not, said the higher-ups. Just shake the tree and keep on shaking for as long as need be. If that required knocking on every door in Tiflis, wasn't that better than admitting they had no actual ideas and no means of narrowing down a list of suspects that numbered in the hundreds? Add to that the fact that the bank robbers were seen as, if not heroes—the death toll and outrageous property damage had ruled that out— then certainly an impressive thorn in the side of a gravely unpopular establishment, and kicking in doors or grilling detainees were jobs Tugushi was grateful to avoid. And if the price was a day spent on his feet seeking for he knew not what, so be it.

However, there was no denying that, once again, his orders erred in the direction of vagueness. "Stop anyone who looks as though they might be suspicious," his commander had told him, in those precise words. Not even *Stop anyone who* is *suspicious*, that would be too straightforward!

Might the pair approaching Tugushi be suspicious? Of course they might, this was Tiflis. Did that mean he ought to be suspicious of them? Tugushi supposed it did. And was he, then, to stop them? There was the ultimate question. Because the man did not belong to a social rank that Tugushi generally concerned himself with, and if the girl perhaps did, she was with the man, and he wouldn't be the first or the last Georgian prince to dally with a bit of stuff beneath his station.

Mind you, Tugushi had no way to prove that the man was a prince, except that he was dressed like one and had the manner of one, and in Tiflis, where minor princes were an embarrassingly common breed, that was as good as a guarantee. Nor had anybody specified that they were to be left alone. But at their most down on their luck, it was hard to conceive of their ilk firing guns and throwing bombs in the middle of Erivansky Square. They were more the sort to cheer from the sidelines. And even if they had no real power, even if they'd frittered away their family's fortune on wine and on women such as the young lady currently swaggering toward Tugushi, there was a risk they'd have influence in some high quarter, enough to make the life of a policeman unpleasant.

Rationalise as he might, the truth was that Tugushi *was* suspicious. The girl seemed faintly familiar; he could have sworn he recognised her as the daughter of a colleague, though it was years since he'd seen her. That was insignificant on its own—what was to say a policeman's daughter wouldn't stray into the bed of some princeling?— but it sufficed to rouse his curiosity, and to make him reflect as to whether the pair weren't being a little too blasé. They'd been ignoring him from the moment they'd stepped into view, and while two weeks before there'd have been nothing odd in that, people tended to be more cognizant of the police these days. Besides, hadn't it been suggested that the criminals might try and leave the city in disguise, as there were rumours that one or more of them had carried out the crime in disguise? And finally, there was the eyepatch the man wore, which fitted perfectly with his ensemble and looked as expensive as the rest of his garments, and yet jogged a stubborn hint of memory.

All the same, Tugushi only knew he'd persuaded himself when he stuck his hand out, at the very last second, nearly cuffing the young woman and having to retreat sharply to avert a collision. Flustered, he overcompensated by barking, "Stop there! Where are you going?"

The prince was nonplussed. "I'm travelling to introduce my fiancée to my parents," he declared, and if he had the manners to omit the *as if it's any of your business* at the end, it was there by implication.

Tugushi would have deserved it. What had he been expecting? Despite the present heightened security, there was no law prohibiting a couple from boarding a train. Likewise, he had no excuse to ask them for papers, never mind a passport, if they were merely going so far as the next station.

Tugushi thought about probing for details—who and where were this family, when was the wedding to take place, that type of thing—and saw immediately how that would make matters worse. If these two were disguised bank robbers, they'd have taken the time to prepare an adequate story, and if, as was vastly more probable, they were what they appeared to be, he'd only make a further fool of himself. Either he needed the courage of his convictions, in which case he'd insist on searching them here on the busy platform, or he'd let them go and hope his intrusion was soon forgotten.

Tugushi's courage had already failed him. Forcing a smile, he said, "Is that so? Then I wish you both the best."

The prince contemplated him as though he were a lunatic, his unveiled eye glinting with disdain. The girl half-heartedly hid a sneer. And Tugushi was still standing in their path, so he sidestepped hastily, allowing the pair to sweep past. Watching their backs, he pondered what his superiors would make of the encounter. Would they be more annoyed that he was accosting the wrong kinds of people, or that, having done so, he'd humiliated himself and accomplished nothing?

Feeling somewhat belligerent and altogether idiotic, he regarded the couple as they proceeded along the platform, conscious all the while that he should be concentrating on identifying some proper suspects. He wished he could quit his fascination with the prince and his alleged bride-to-be—and what an obvious lie that was, the girl was too unashamedly pretty and sure of herself to be taken home to meet even the most liberal parents! What if they should catch him staring? Fights had started in Tiflis over slighter indiscretions, and there was no promise that his uniform would protect him. And still he was fixated, as he silently cursed himself.

Maybe he was simply justifying his behaviour, but didn't they seem fractionally less confident now? And for all his debonairness, the man walked stiffly, like he'd been injured and was trying to obscure the debility. The woman, meanwhile, was sashaying in a frankly provocative fashion, but almost exaggeratedly so. Could her display be in part to camouflage some genuine inconvenience? The more Tugushi looked, the more he felt that, if you dismissed the mood of self-absorbed casualness they were projecting, there was something definitely awry about them.

As he thought it, an object fell from inside the woman's skirts. Tugushi's impulse was to glance away politely, and he reminded himself how preposterous that would be, but the moment the woman realised what had happened, she bent to pick the stray thing up. Tugushi had the briefest instant to see, and even then he was squinting, distracted by his sense of propriety. For all that, he was positive that what the woman's gloved fingers were closing around, what had tumbled from some concealed pouch in her undergarments, was a wad of banknotes.

"Hey!" Tugushi cried, but not loudly. He was too uncertain to draw anyone else's notice, especially that of his colleagues farther down the platform. He began to trot toward the couple, half convinced they would run—though with the train not yet arrived, they had nowhere to run to—and somehow disappointed when they didn't.

By the time he caught them up, they'd turned to face him. Again, he didn't know what he'd expected, but their response wasn't that of malefactors who'd been found out. The prince was as haughty as ever, the girl wore a teasing smirk, and Tugushi's every instinct was to leave them to their affairs. If rich eccentrics held that the ideal place to store their funds was in their knickers, did he have a right to argue with them?

"What's that you have there?" Tugushi asked, attempting not to sound contrite.

He'd addressed his enquiry to the woman, but it was her partner who answered. "You mean here?" he said.

His eye was lowered, as though hunting for his own hand, which was tucked into a pocket of his extravagant coat. But the bulge there couldn't possibly be accounted for by a hand alone, not unless it contained something hard and bulky that was pointed upward into Tugushi's face.

Before his initial shiver of panic could take hold, the woman spoke, and her tone was deeper than he'd have anticipated, less girlish and more assured. "Or did you mean this?" she wondered.

Tugushi dragged his gaze sideways, and now he was looking at the woman's hand. Her glove was embroidered with white lace patterned in designs of roses and lilies, and her wrist and exposed fingers were lily-white as well, and peculiarly, those observations seemed to him as important as the stack of notes bound in a slip of paper that lay in her palm. Perhaps it was solely that he didn't want to think about them, didn't want to estimate their worth.

But it was too late. And if mathematics had never been his strongest suit, nevertheless he felt safe in saying that the total far exceeded what he'd earn in a year.

It seemed to Tugushi that an entire minute had gone by since he'd stopped the pair, and at the same time he acknowledged that it couldn't be more than five seconds. He was simultaneously afraid that he was attracting attention and aware that he ought to be doing precisely that. And likely someone would have taken an interest in what the three of them were up to, were it not for the chugging clamour that had engulfed the station, signalling the advent of the train that most of those gathered were awaiting.

He need only call out, before his words were drowned in that mechanical uproar. He need only shout, *Here they are, two of the bank robbers!* and half a dozen other policemen would descend on them. Did he really believe this man would shoot him in front of a panoply of witnesses?

Yes. Yes, he did. The expression in his eye said he would, and that he'd do so without a twinge of conscience. Tugushi had met killers in his days, and he was in the company of one now. The woman, too; this close, he could discern her whole violent history, as though it were an acrid scent mixed in with her heavy perfume. If he gave them away, his reward would be a bullet in the gut.

And if he didn't?

The train was visible behind the couple—the fake couple, rather—and Tugushi made himself practically cross-eyed by trying to track its last approach while not losing sight of both the gun and the money, those two objects that represented the choice he had to make. The train's whistle sounded. He sensed that bodies were clustering toward them; the train had happened to come to rest so that they were in the way of one of its doors.

His time was up. Tugushi reached out, plucked the wad of notes from the woman's palm, and slid it neatly into a pocket. "Enjoy your journey, sir and madam," he said, "and I hope married life suits you well."

TWENTY

THROUGH NO CHOICE of his own, Doctor Jacob Zhitomirsky's existence had become more complicated than he could ever have imagined or desired. He woke to each fresh dawn with trepidation, out of nebulous nightmares. He felt himself to be an insect struggling vainly in a web he was unable to see the edges of. Surrounded by too many threats, he tried to dread them all equally, fearful that whichever he failed to focus on would be the one that eventually caught up with him.

Such was the life of a revolutionary, he supposed. And at least he had the comfort of knowing he wasn't paranoid. The threats were real. The web was real. He genuinely was trapped, and no amount of struggling would free him.

All of this flashed across Zhitomirsky's mind when he heard the knock at his door, not as thoughts but as a single, black rush of sensation. Was this the day they came for him? Was this the nudge that tipped him into the abyss? The trembling in the base of his stomach assured him that it was. But one unusual consequence of living in perpetual fear was that he hardly let it perturb him anymore, and so his demeanour was every bit a professional's as he opened the door.

The effort was wasted. The dishevelled figure on its other side barely glanced at him before shoving his way inside. "Doctor Zhitomirsky?" his visitor queried, once within the apartment. "Indeed you are, I know a medical man when I see one! Do you mind if I take a seat? I've been travelling for... hell, longer than I can remember. They said you'd be expecting me?"

By that time, the visitor had already dropped into a chair with a satisfied grunt. Zhitomirsky noticed, however, that for all his show of nonchalance, he'd been careful to keep the cumbersome suitcase he'd brought with him close at hand.

It was true, Zhitomirsky *had* been expecting him, though not today and not with any particular conviction that he'd materialise. Zhitomirsky had been keeping his fingers crossed that his guest might get himself arrested en route and refrain from becoming yet another strand in that binding web. "You're Ter-Petrosian, aren't you?"

The man grinned affably. "But call me Kamo, everybody does."

Zhitomirsky didn't want to call him Kamo. He had no wish to call anyone by their *nom de guerre*. "And you're here about the eye. Yes, I had a letter."

Belatedly he noted that Ter-Petrosian—Kamo, damn

it—was wearing an eyepatch. To be fair, he seemed the sort who might do so from affectation as much as necessity. The letter, which had come from Lenin a week earlier, had intimated that his injury was trivial, and self-inflicted, and would have healed by now had it been properly ministered to in the first place. Further, Lenin had remarked that Zhitomirsky's patient-to-be was a revolutionary hero and deserved better treatment from his comrades than he'd received, which Zhitomirsky had taken as a polite way of dancing around the insinuation that nobody would be paying him for his work.

Well, that was what it meant to be a physician to Bolsheviks, and probably it was worthwhile practice for the day they succeeded in their revolution and rewrote the world according to the laws of Marx and Engels. At any rate, there was no use in grumbling, not when he had considerably bigger issues to concern him, like the fact that the notorious savage Kamo, one of the perpetrators of the Tiflis bank heist, was in his apartment and demanding his attention.

"I'll get my bag," Zhitomirsky said. "Can I offer you a drink?"

"I've never turned down a drink," Kamo replied, and Zhitomirsky could easily believe him.

He hurried through into his bedroom, where he kept a bag always ready for emergencies, and then on to the kitchen, to pour two glasses of vodka from the bottle he had stashed there, which he retained for medical purposes and also for occasional self-medication. He carried the glasses back into the main room in his free hand and placed them both on the coffee table in front of the chair in which Kamo was sprawled.

"It's swill," he said apologetically. "You'd think it would be feasible in so grand a city as this to buy decent vodka, but no."

Yet Kamo was looking at him not the glasses, with calculating curiosity. "Aren't you somewhat young to be a doctor?" he asked.

Aren't you young to be a bank robber and a killer? Zhitomirsky thought. He guessed they were roughly the same age. "I'm qualified. But if you'd sooner I refer you to an older colleague, I know of one or two who might be available." *Though since they're not loyal comrades, they'd prefer to be paid in actual currency rather than dim promises of a nobler future.*

Kamo shook his head lazily. "You'll do. One doctor's as good as any other to me." He peeled up the eyepatch. "And time heals all wounds, isn't that so?"

Zhitomirsky let the implied dismissal of his entire trade go. After all, his visitor's own injury showed how wrong he was: time had done his wound no favours. It had healed, but it had healed badly, and the scarring was an ugly mess.

"Allow me to make a proper inspection," he proposed.

"You do that," Kamo agreed charitably. He sighed. "I'm happy to be off my feet. I've scarcely had a minute's rest since I left Lenin and that fine upstanding wife of his. Quite a summer it's been! I'd gladly have stayed longer, you can't imagine the fuss they made of me. It's remarkable what a little matter of three hundred thousand or so roubles does for people's opinion of you."

But Zhitomirsky *could* imagine. There had been

enough talk of that amount, and of its vanishment and possible whereabouts, and of the authorities' repeated failure to locate it, that the haul had acquired an almost mythical status, like some antediluvian treasure. The list of those who would have been fascinated to overhear this conversation included the populations of several countries, and even now the general interest was only beginning to die down.

However, for numerous reasons, Zhitomirsky had no inclination to think about money. Instead, he concentrated on his patient's injured eye, manoeuvring his brow gently with the fingers of one hand so as to get the best of the drab afternoon daylight leaking between the curtains. If the orb could never be made perfectly right, minor surgery would undo some of the damage that neglect and incompetent doctoring had wreaked.

He had hoped to get this over with today. But to his frustration, it was evident that he'd need to make preparations that went beyond what he had in the apartment. And he would have said as much, had his visitor been less engaged by the sound of his own voice.

"Of course," Kamo rambled, "they have to be nice to me, to the great expropriator of Tiflis, but the truth is that we did nothing except waste our time and break a few windows. Most of the cash is of no damned use to Lenin or to anyone else. They recorded the serial numbers on the larger notes, and every bank in Europe and America is on the lookout for them. Good old Koba had his moles inside the banking office, but obviously they never thought to mention that!"

He chuckled. He seemed legitimately amused by the

notion that he and his companions had risked their lives to procure funds for the party that no-one dared spend, and if Zhitomirsky hadn't immediately pegged him as a maniac, that would have done it.

"But none of that's important now," Kamo went on. "I've an infinitely bigger job in mind. One so big that, by the end of the year, nobody will remember that the Tiflis bank was robbed." He patted the case beside him. "See this? It's crammed full of two hundred detonators, along with other bits and pieces for the amateur bomb maker. And I intend to put it all to exceptional use."

Zhitomirsky managed not to let on how weak his knees had become at the news that he was standing next to a case filled with bomb-making equipment, which Kamo had just heartily patted as if it were a faithful hound.

"Is that so?" he said, because he felt Kamo required some response, and commended himself for delivering the words without a quaver.

"It is. You know what I've realised, doctor? Everyone else has come to Europe, and there must be a reason. If even Lenin hasn't the courage to go back home, wouldn't I be an idiot to? They say the Okhrana reaches everywhere, but I don't believe that, and the police here are like lambs. Do you know I've been travelling all this time on a borrowed passport? A wanted man, toting around a case full of detonators, pockets weighted with stolen banknotes, and with a passport that any cretin could tell isn't his, yet I go where I please and no-one tries to stop me."

"Yes," Zhitomirsky said, "perhaps you're correct." He was consumed by a desperate craving that Kamo should desist from talking. "Myself, I feel a great deal safer here than I would in Russia," he added, though nothing could have been less true. "And as for your eye, it's never going to be good as new, but I can certainly help. I'll need a brief while to prepare for the operation. If you can return in a couple of days, I'll see to it."

Kamo frowned. "A couple of days? I suppose I can."

Zhitomirsky fought to hide his relief. He'd been anxious that Kamo would either insist that he operate straight away or, worse, that he'd been expecting to be put up, detonator-filled suitcase and all. "Then how about Friday?" he suggested.

Kamo clasped the nearest glass of vodka, which he'd thus far ignored, drained it in a single gulp, slapped the glass back on the table with a resounding *clink*, and hopped to his feet. He caught up his case as carelessly as though it were packed with rags. "Friday it is."

Zhitomirsky saw him to the door and they said their goodbyes. If Kamo was aggravated at having come all this way for no purpose, or worried over where he'd spend the night—or, indeed, bothered by anything whatsoever—it would have been impossible to guess from the cheerfulness with which he departed, his suitcase with its lethal potential tucked casually under one arm.

The doctor waited until Kamo's footsteps had faded, then waited for a minute or so more, and then admitted to himself that he was only waiting because he didn't want to act, and hastened to the telephone in its alcove.

Not many people had telephones in the city. They had stipulated that he should, and his profession had made its appearance less strange. Still, he despised the device, as he despised everything to do with them, and as, in this moment, he despised himself. Nevertheless, he picked up the receiver, and when the operator answered, gave the name he'd been told to give, which he assumed to be fake.

As the crackling on the line subsided, a male voice he didn't recognise said, "*Yes?*"

"It's Doctor Zhitomirsky."

"*Yes,*" the voice reiterated. The speaker didn't give the impression of much caring who he was, but that was all part of the show. He was meant to think they were busy every second of every day in fielding calls from those like him, their vast network of agents and informers.

Zhitomirsky had grown used to such unsubtle manipulation. It was five years since the Okhrana had approached him, back when he was a student, and had turned him effortlessly with a few well-placed threats, together with that most special of promises, protection. While he belonged to them, he'd be safe.

It was the oldest lie in the book. For sure, he was safe from the Okhrana, so long as he was useful and so long as he didn't fall foul of an administrative error or change in command. But from his fellow Bolsheviks? After what he did today, and all his past betrayals that were poised to come to light? No such security could exist.

But that was the web he was snared in, and wriggle as he might, it was too late to escape. "That man you've been looking for?" Zhitomirsky said. "Yes... yes... Ter-Petrosian. He's in Berlin. He's been to my apartment, and he'll be here again. I can confirm he's carrying bomb-making equipment, that he's travelling under a false passport, and that he's planning another job in the city. There won't be a better chance than this."

He heard scribbling at the other end of the line, barely perceptible above the underlying crushed-paper crackle. Then the voice said, "*Duly noted. We'll be in touch, doctor.*" And the line went dead.

Zhitomirsky put down the receiver. What would happen now? But the specifics didn't matter, not for him. Because if he hadn't already been damned, this would have done it. He had just denounced the hero of the Tiflis bank robbery, the cause célèbre of the Bolshevik party. And this time there was no way the man would be wriggling free of the punishment that awaited him— which, given the immensity of his crimes and the copious blood on his hands, would inevitably mean death.

EPILOGUE

KAMO WAS INORDINATELY fond of his bicycle. Moreover, he was so convinced that it was in perfect accord with his personality that he half imagined the contraption might have been invented expressly for him. He didn't care that there were those who thought he looked ridiculous; better, after all, to look ridiculous and for people to underestimate you.

He joked that his was the only bicycle in the whole of Tiflis, but for all he knew he was right. The machine was profoundly ill-fitted to the city's ancient cobbled streets, and his trips routinely left him bruised and aching. Again, he couldn't have cared less. There was something about the sensation, about moving so much faster than he could unassisted and yet entirely under his own steam. It was superior to riding a horse, or even in a motorcar. With his bicycle, he'd found an unprecedented freedom, and the dismayed scowls and jeers he received as he hurtled by served solely to enhance his pleasure.

More than that, and despite the hazardous energies that still burned in him, Kamo felt that it had brought him a sort of peace. Or maybe his favourite mode of transport was a symptom of a wider change that had occurred in him. Here, back in his homeland, he had come to an end of his wanderings, so many of which had been forced upon him.

He was glad to have put Russia and the capital behind him. Life there hadn't suited him. Actually, it had inspired the worst in him, and if he'd seen that, others must have too. Hadn't it been Koba who'd suggested he return? Of course, he wasn't Koba anymore, he was Stalin now, but Kamo couldn't quite accept that new name. Did he really picture himself to be a man of steel? It was he, Kamo, who'd been the steely one, the doer, the killer when there was killing to be done. Then again, he conceded that it might be a different kind of steeliness Koba had named himself for, a representation of the willpower that had propelled him to where he was, at the summit of the magnificent construct that was the Soviet Union.

At any rate, Kamo should have decamped before he did, and before he was asked to. Perhaps he'd believed his own legends, or had been naive enough to suppose that being a legendary bandit hero would carry more cache than it ever could have. When events moved at such an incredible pace, you could find yourself becoming a dinosaur in the blink of an eye, a discomforting relic of an age that had left too many skeletons in too many closets.

Certainly, he'd let his enthusiasm get the better of him. Doubtless it had seemed a sensible decision to grant Kamo command of a special forces unit during the civil war that had erupted in the immediate wake of the revolution, and Kamo himself had considered it so. He'd taken to the role like a fish to water, or rather, like a wolf to the hunt. He'd been given a free rein; it had been in the nature of those times that nobody watched anyone's actions too closely, since there was always the risk of seeing some sight you'd regret. And so Kamo had done things his own way, bringing to bear his considerable experience as doer of distasteful but necessary jobs. Yet he'd missed the days of the Outfit, had missed having the likes of Anneta, Patsia, and Alexandra around. It had never been easy to know who you could trust, but in a nation at war with itself, it became all the harder.

He'd been obliged to modify his methods accordingly. He had devised a test, which he'd regarded as foolproof. When he was sent new recruits, whether or not he had reason to doubt them, he'd wake them in the blackest hours of the night and would drag them out to be shot, as though they'd been captured by the troops of the White Army. If their reaction was stubborn bravery and fortitude, they'd earned themselves a place in his unit. If their reaction was cowardice, he would put a bullet in them right there on the spot.

And once, in his zeal, he'd gone further. It was tough, in retrospect, to piece together thought processes that had been hurled into whirling fragments by hunger, exhaustion, and the interminable stresses of warfare, but what he'd done had seemed rational in the moment. He had drawn his knife, hacked open the dead man's chest, sliced out his heart, and proffered it to the nearest soldier, declaring cheerfully, "Here is the heart of your officer!"

Even then, the deed might have passed for one more horror in an age in which horrors were abundantly common, except that the soldier in question, Fyodor Alliluyev, did not at all have Kamo's sound constitution and lackadaisical approach to death. His mind had snapped with astonishing abruptness, and so far as Kamo knew, he hadn't uttered a word since. And even *that* would indubitably have gone down as another petty tragedy of a tragic era, were it not for the fact that Fyodor Alliluyev was brother to Nadya Alliluyeva, who was second wife to one Joseph Stalin.

That had definitely proven awkward. In fairness, Stalin had taken it well, and Kamo had suspected he'd seen the funny side. And there had been enough else going on that the matter had vanished from everyone's attentions quite rapidly, though pitiful, lily-livered Fyodor was still in the hospital, trapped inside the dark chasms of his own appalled brain.

Troubled at the recollection, Kamo picked up speed, recklessly ignoring how close he was to the caravansary and that he was heading into the busiest areas of town. He threaded among pedestrians and carts, horses and the odd burdened camel, shouting "Hey!" or "Watch it, idiot!" whenever anybody threatened to get in his way. The bicycle shook and rattled beneath him, feeling at every instant as if it might collapse, and that only heightened his delight. He was at once the master of his own destiny and hopelessly out of control. The breeze ruffled his hair and tugged at his clothing, the sounds and scents of Tiflis washed over him, and it seemed just possible that, if he could spin his feet sufficiently fast, he might outride the past.

A foolish whim, and foolish, in part, because he didn't really mean it. He had no genuine desire to rid himself of the old Kamo, who he'd learned to view as like a tatty, violently tempered lion in a circus cage, glowering out at him from between the bars. If he were truthful, it entertained him to stare on occasions into that dim enclosure and marvel at what he found there.

It hadn't occurred to him at the time, nor until months after, that there was anything unusual in cutting a man's heart from his chest. That had been the truly disturbing revelation: not that there might be something wrong with his behaviour, but that he'd never contemplated the possibility until suddenly he did. And he'd felt no sympathy for Fyodor Alliluyev, no understanding either, which was strange given how much of his life Kamo had spent locked up in hospitals and asylums. Indeed, his experiences had made him *less* sympathetic, since they weren't a similarity but an unassailable point of difference. Fyodor had been weak and so had gone mad. Kamo had been strong and hadn't.

That was what he'd believed, and for the majority of his lengthy imprisonment in the years prior to the revolution, it was what they'd believed too, the doctors, the lawyers, the politicians, the journalists, the idle spectators, the multitudes who'd deigned to furnish their opinions on his mental health. But the doctors had been the most shrewd and cynical. They'd told him he was feigning his madness and that no-one could do so for long: a few weeks, a couple of months at best. Kamo had agreed with them on the first score and disagreed vehemently on the second. Yes, his madness was a fabrication, and what he knew that they didn't was that it was also a protracted and complex game, played more for his own amusement than to keep his neck from the noose.

His game had a handful of simple rules. Originality was foremost. He'd refused to let his performance grow drab, or to let them imagine they had a handle on his condition. One day he'd complain of fictitious vermin keeping him awake with their scurrying through the walls, the next he'd assume an invented persona, and then for a week he'd sink into a silence so acute that they'd start to convince themselves he'd been struck dumb—as poor Fyodor Alliluyev would be a decade later.

For Kamo to win his game, he need only abide until they gave up in despair of comprehending him, never mind curing him, or until they abandoned their hypocritical moralising and consented to execute a lunatic, the indignation of hand-wringing milksops be damned. He'd quickly come to acknowledge that he might prefer the latter outcome. Incarceration at the Tsar's convenience was a tiresome business, even incarceration as a maniac, and even when his stay was spiced with the ingenious tortures that his custodians were sure would compel him to admit his deception. Kamo, who had such a low capacity for pain that he honestly couldn't conceive of how anyone got worked up over it, had endured their efforts with equanimity, as just another aspect of the game.

Still, the ordeal had worn on him. It was dull when the

one person interested in your amusement was you, and when his vigour had flagged—as inevitably happened sometimes—there had been nobody, and the boredom was far worse than some dolt sticking needles under his nails. Boredom alone could make a madman out of you if you weren't careful, and if he'd let it, how could he have feigned being mad? Preferable to swing from a rope than to lose the game.

That all seemed so long ago. His escape, his recapture, the time when they'd finally decided they'd had enough and that it was overdue he died for his many and varied crimes, and his ludicrous last-minute pardon thanks to the celebrations for the accursed Romanov family's tricentennial, all of that had the air of a tall tale he'd constructed himself. He'd recited plenty of such stories, though few of them about his years of imprisonment. But wasn't it plausible that, neglected and bottled inside him, the facts really had distorted into some absurd fantasy?

Perhaps. Because now Kamo looked back and wondered if they hadn't been right from the beginning. Maybe sane men didn't cut other men's hearts out while they were still warm and offer them as gifts. Maybe he hadn't ever been feigning madness. Or maybe he had and hadn't been able to keep it up, as they'd assured him he wouldn't, and somewhere along the line he'd become an insane man deluding himself that he was sane so that he could persuade others he was insane. Wasn't that a funny notion?

But this avenue of speculation was destroying his good mood and detracting from his one great joy in life, and so, with a degree of difficulty, Kamo stifled it. The conclusion he came to was the same he always arrived at: that none of these questions mattered. They didn't matter to him, they didn't matter to anyone else, and probably the universe was equally indifferent. Mad or sane, he'd ended up where he was, and he was fortunate in that he liked that place fine. What was the use in worrying?

All this while, he hadn't been paying any heed to his course, except for the minimum that was necessary to avoid running someone over or crashing into obstacles. But then, his daily rides invariably took more or less the same route, a habit he'd slipped into precisely so that he'd never have to give them too much consideration. He had raced through the centre of the city, and now was on a street almost bereft of traffic.

Almost, but not quite. There was a single vehicle, a hulking truck, approaching from the opposite direction. Later than he should have, he realised the truck was coming toward him and that it was coming too fast. He hadn't known there were any such vehicles in the city. *The only truck and the only bicycle in Tiflis*, Kamo thought, *and we're rushing straight at each other.*

He tried to swerve, unaccountably certain that the attempt would be futile. Sure enough, the driver mirrored his movement, so that they were still set to collide and all he'd accomplished was to waste a vital second. Didn't he recognise the man behind the wheel? Kamo felt that he did. But he couldn't put a name to the face, could merely say that he was somebody he'd encountered: a fellow revolutionary, no doubt, a local or one of the countless hangers-on who'd flocked around the party headquarters.

It made sense. Kamo had often predicted that he'd die at the hand of someone he knew. And ultimately this man was just that, a hand. The mind that controlled him was an entire country away. Kamo couldn't bring himself to blame his friend. He couldn't bring himself to feel much of anything, besides perhaps for a glimmer of relief. To Koba, who had become Stalin, his was simply another name to be crossed off an extensive list. This was nothing personal.

And that was the spirit in which he'd meet death, Kamo determined. He was glad that he could, glad he'd lost so many crucial parts of his faculties that dying seemed like a jaunt into the unknown. Here he was, where he'd grown up, where he'd taken ample lives of his own, not far from the spot where he'd made history, his end ordered by a comrade he'd joked with on these very streets. So what?

The truck struck his bicycle like a bull colliding with a sapling, and Kamo was conscious of a terrific jolt and of being dragged through the air. But not of pain; his uncanny immunity was serving him well, even at the last. The world spun and was still, the sound of the truck rose in a crescendo and then faded to absolute quiet.

Nothing personal. One more accident on the path to the future he'd fought and killed and stolen for. Kamo would lie here, devoid of pain, enjoying his momentary peace. And the revolution would go on, to whatever grand heights or grotesque depths it chose to explore, without this mad old bank robber surviving to clog up the gears.

AFTERWORD

MY ONE WORRY when editor David Thomas Moore approached me with the concept of writing a short novel based on the 1907 Tiflis bank robbery was whether there'd be enough material there to spin a novel, even a short novel, out of. We're so used to phrases like "Based on Historical Events" meaning something closer to "People with the same names as these characters really lived and did vaguely similar things, except one of them had died by this point and another was thirty years younger and also the events we've crammed into a week took place over the course of eighteen months." And among the reasons for that generally high level of inaccuracy is that history doesn't much care for the poor writer who tries to dramatize its bewildering tangles years or decades or centuries later. History, as a rule, tends to be a right old mess, and its drama a different sort to that which fits neatly between book covers or the credits of a movie.

With that in mind, I wouldn't at all blame the sceptical reader who spent their time with this book wishing the author couldn't stick to the facts and keep from embellishing them with so many implausible eccentricities. However, in this case, they'd be wrong: almost everything you've just read, no matter how incredible or absurd, is as faithful to the known history as I could make it. So yes, to pick an obvious example, the future Joseph Stalin really did recruit a banking office insider via an admiration of his youthful poetry, and they really did have their fateful discussion over a glass of milk.

It actually turns out to be easier to list what I cut from whole cloth rather than what I didn't, since there's a total of one scene where I strayed deliberately from what's known or believed to have occurred. While the essential elements of the chapter they appear in are genuine, it's unlikely to have been Mikha and Maro Bochoridze who delivered the mattress full of stolen cash to the Tiflis observatory; what mention we have refers to the deed being undertaken by porters. And the policeman Tugushi, who runs afoul of Kamo and one of his gunslinger girls, is the sole named character in the book that I invented, though again, the details surrounding his encounter are heavily based in reality.

In the end, then, my bigger concern was an overabundance of good material, and the question of what to cut when there was so much I'd have loved to incorporate. Reducing Kamo's post-heist misadventures to a handful of paragraphs in the epilogue, for example, was heart-breaking, and I clearly remember the day I realised that to include them properly wouldn't be feasible. And there as elsewhere, the pressure was more to try and rationalise the improbabilities than to concoct drama where there wasn't any: Kamo, frankly, deserves an entire book to himself. Of course, the same could be said for Koba, but unsurprisingly, many a historian and author has got there already. For those who'd like to know more about the years that shaped him into one of the twentieth century's most savage and contradictory figures, I'd heartily recommend Simon Montefiore's *Young Stalin*, a superb work of history and biography that was invaluable in the writing of this novel.

Lastly, a few thank yous: to David Thomas Moore, for offering me one of the more fascinating and challenging projects I've ever had the good fortune to be involved with; to Professors Maggie Tallerman and George Hewitt for their advice and guidance; to Hanaa at JSTOR for her kind assistance; to my indispensable beta reader Tom Rice; and, as always, to my friends and family for their enthusiasm and support.

David Tallerman

FIND US ONLINE!

www.rebellionpublishing.com

/rebellionpub   /rebellionpublishing   /rebellionpublishing

SIGN UP TO OUR NEWSLETTER!

rebellionpublishing.com/newsletter

YOUR REVIEWS MATTER!

Enjoy this book? Got something to say?

Leave a review on Amazon, GoodReads or with your
favourite bookseller and let the world know!